I0538400

# Spider's Lifeline

## Book 3 of the Pipe Woman's Legacy

Lynne Cantwell

hearth/myth

*a hearth/myth book*

# Table of Contents

Chapter 1 ...................................................................................... 1

Chapter 2 ...................................................................................... 9

The big sister speaks ................................................................. 19

Chapter 3 .................................................................................... 23

Chapter 4 .................................................................................... 38

Chapter 5 .................................................................................... 45

Chapter 6 .................................................................................... 57

Two weeks earlier. . . .................................................................. 73

Chapter 7 .................................................................................... 81

Chapter 8 .................................................................................... 93

While Webb was calming Hilary down. . . ........................... 105

Chapter 9 .................................................................................. 117

While Webb was talking about cake. . . .............................. 131

Chapter 10 ................................................................................ 138

Chapter 11 ................................................................................ 153

Chapter 12 ................................................................................ 161

Author's Note ........................................................................... 175

About the Author ..................................................................... 176

# Chapter 1

I'm sure you've heard that it's a bad idea to bargain with the gods. That's true. However, it is possible to misdirect Them. And sometimes – if you're careful, and not a little bit lucky – you can even out-Trick a Trickster.

Of course, it helps if you, too, are a Trickster, and luckily, I am. I'm Webb Curtis, the somewhat famous *heyoka* to his famous sister Sage's Thunderbird. Sage's schtick was saving the world; I was supposed to make her way smoother by speaking truth to power. Now, you can speak truth to power by employing a couple of different strategies: either you can turn everything into a joke, thereby becoming an annoying pain in the ass; or you can lay out the facts, and challenge everyone involved to come up with a solution that not only fits the situation but also benefits everybody – or as close to everybody as you can manage.

Option Two is my mother's strategy. I'm sure you've heard of her: Naomi Witherspoon Curtis. No? The mediator who talked Jehovah into sharing power with the ancient gods and goddesses whose worship He displaced? She wrote a book about her experience. Several books, in fact. She was pregnant with Sage in the last book. No? Come on – history class, then. It was a big deal when the gods came back to Earth. I know we talked about it when *I* was in school – and not just because my family was involved. Sure, it was local history, more or less, but the world was in an upheaval for at least a decade afterward.

Seriously? What do they teach kids these days, anyway?

So, then, you also never heard about how the gods solved the problem of climate change after my sister and her boyfriend, Rafe Orloff, kicked Their butts into gear. Well, that's good to hear. I'll have to let her know that her fifteen minutes of fame are up. I'm sure she'll be grateful. She never wanted to be famous, anyway.

But basically what you're telling me is that you have no idea how we got where we are today: a world in which the gods insist that we humans have to be nice to one another; that we share with those less fortunate, and innovate for more than just money; that everyone has enough to eat, clothes on their backs, a decent home, educational opportunities, access to health care; that we don't scam each other; that we don't discriminate based on skin color or faith or age or gender or any of those things. I mean, I know you don't *remember* a time when all that nasty stuff happened, because *I* don't remember it, and I'm thirty-five. But my parents remember, and my grandparents did, and Sage and I certainly heard about it from them.

And believe it or not, as great as life on Earth is now, there are always some Neanderthals who want to take us back to the bad old days, so they can be in charge. It's part of human nature, I guess. Although sometimes the Neanderthals are gods, and when that's the case, things can get pretty Tricky.

I hadn't had to resort to Option One – i.e., annoying pain in the ass – in many years. After the gods got busy on fixing the climate, life on Earth calmed down a lot. The gods had Their hands full with implementing the strategy Rafe had developed, and that gave the rest of us a breather. My family had space to mourn the passing of my great-grandfather, Looks Far Guzmán, and celebrate some weddings.

My parents' best friends, George Lofton and Shannon McDonough – Uncle George and Aunt Shannon to Sage and me – tied the knot a year and a day after Grandfather's death.

And Sage and Rafe got married right after they finished their master's degrees at the University of Colorado. Then they moved to Washington, D.C., to work for a shadowy quasi-governmental agency that was less interested in their educational credentials than in their magical powers.

Whereas their classmate, Hilary Takahashi, and I found we were more interested in each other than in our own magical powers, and moved in together. Hilary even turned down an offer from the agency where Sage and Rafe work to stay here in Colorado with me. I had mixed feelings about that. Don't get me wrong – I love Hilary. But she has mathematical and computer-programming abilities far beyond those of most mortal men and women, and she could have been making quite a lucrative living elsewhere. Instead, she was working for CU – staff, not teaching – while I muddled around, trying to make a name for myself in the arts.

I'm a fiber artist. Knitting is my superpower.

That's only partly a joke.

What it meant in practical terms was that, at the age of thirty-five, I was still basically living on my parents' sufferance. We were still living in the just-off-campus house in Boulder that my parents bought and fixed up when Sage went off to college. Sage, Rafe, and Hilary were already living there when I moved in during my freshman year, and inertia kept Hilary and me there when Sage and Rafe left for the East Coast. It made sense from a financial standpoint; we could never have afforded anything in Boulder on one salary. I mean, when the gods decreed that everyone would have decent housing, They didn't mean everybody would get a mansion – or even a single-family house in a pricey area within walking distance from work. But inertia had also kept us there long past the point when we should have gotten our own place.

My parents were okay with it. A few years earlier, Dad and Uncle George had even helped me knock out a wall and extend the back bedroom, so I could have a studio similar to the one I had in high school when I was still living at home. Uncle George had also helped me put in a backyard deck with a pond for Enkou, Hilary's kappa, although her personal ninja turtle still seemed to prefer the creek. Dad also put new appliances in the kitchen for us, and we had upgraded the furniture from College Dumpster Deluxe. But none of it changed the fact that I was thirty-five years old and still renting from my parents.

First world problems, as they say. Funny how that stuff becomes less important when the fate of the Earth is at stake.

My first clue was a nightmare I had one chilly October night in 2051. It had still been warm when we went to bed, and we'd forgotten to close the window all the way. But the temperature had dropped overnight, and my sleep was wracked with visions of deep blue ice palaces peopled with hatchet-faced blonds, all of them looking at me expectantly, as if it was my job to fix whatever was bothering them. Their gazes turned menacing as I walked past them, bewildered, with my shoulders hunched against the cold. They began to follow me, and I began to run, trying not to trip on the patchy ice that served as a road or path.

I flinched as a smirking voice beside me said, "It begins." I recognized the voice, although I couldn't place its owner. But I never got a chance to see who it was – because as I turned toward the speaker, a massive being, shrouded in smoke, captured my attention by blocking my path.

"Yes! Run!" this new being cackled. "Run fast and run far! For you will never escape me, and it pleases me to see you try!"

"Who are you?" I cried out, or thought I did, the way one does in dreams.

"You know me, little web-maker," the smoke-being said. "We have tangled before, and will do so again ere all is through. I have taken the measure of your talents, and found you wanting. This time, I shall prevail!" The being then lunged at me. I cowered as it shredded and broke around me. Its vicious laughter still rang in my ears as I awoke.

I sat up, breathing hard, and ran a hand across the back of my neck; the dream had made me sweat for real, and my skin was rapidly turning clammy. I glanced at the open window and thought the temperature had *really* dropped overnight; ice crystals had formed on the screen.

Shivering, and taking care not to wake Hilary, I got up to close the window. But by the time I got there, the frost had melted away.

I am, as I've said, *heyoka*, a Sacred Clown; I live backwards, or more accurately, I know what will happen in the future and how we will get there. Unless events pertain to me, in which case whatever vision I've been granted typically turns out to be useless. I learn enough to know that something big will happen – just not how it will all go down.

Of all the ways, over the years, that I have learned about the future, nightmares are just about my least favorite. I shut the window, kissed Hilary's temple, slipped on a sweatshirt, and quietly let myself out the back door.

A not-quite-quarter moon spread its light over the deck and reflected in the still surface of the pond. I could tell at a glance that Enkou wasn't there. Probably for the best, I thought. At least he and Hilary would be rested. I was pretty sure I wouldn't sleep any more that night.

Three chairs lined the edge of the deck facing the pond. I took the middle one and propped my feet up on the railing. Then I took a deep breath and closed my eyes. I needed more information about what I'd just seen in my dream, and following events in the timestream was the most reliable way I knew to get it.

The timestream is my own creation – a simulation, if you will, of the web of life – and sinking into it is a lot like diving into a large body of water. There are an almost infinite number of currents, some competing, most running parallel or coming nowhere near any others. My cousin Leonard, who's a Wolf Dreamer for the Lakota Sioux, taught me how to make timestreams. He told me once that it's easy for some people to go astray in them, although I've never had a problem – probably because of who I am.

Anyway, I had just found the part of the stream I wanted – I could tell because a strand of bright light, like a laser beam, had appeared below me – and was about to follow it to its conclusion when I heard movement on the deck to my left. Sighing, I dropped the path of light and allowed myself to surface to *now*. Then I turned my head to see what was going on. If it was Enkou, the Japanese water demon and I were going to have words.

It wasn't Enkou.

A bundle of tangled black hair and red blanket rose from the shadowed corner where the short end of the L of the deck met the house. As the moonlight touched His features, I dropped my feet to the deck. "Iktomi?" I asked. This was getting weirder by the second. The Lakota spider god was my patron, nominally, but I had rarely encountered Him in human form. And when I had, He had had a mischievous air befitting a Trickster. On this night, however, He looked less mischievous than mysterious. Sinister, almost.

"You don't need to do that time-travel stuff," He said, His voice raspy. "I'll tell you what's going on."

"So tell me," I said.

"The agreement is breaking down."

"The mediation?"

He nodded impatiently. "It's going to be god against god before long," He said, "and Earth will be the final battleground. Just like before."

"Like *when* before?" I thought I knew the answer, but that answer terrified me.

He opened His mouth – to kid me about being dense, maybe – but then He glanced aside and hunched back toward the shadows. "Tell your mother," He said.

"Tell her what?"

"TELL HER!" He roared, His voice shredding on the night air – reminding me so forcefully of the smoke being in my nightmare that I shuddered. Hunching my own shoulders, I hurried toward the corner where He'd been – to shake a better answer out of Him, maybe, as if that ever worked with the gods. But He was gone.

As I straightened, I caught sight of a spider web anchored by the railing, the house wall, and the corner where the two structures met. Frost, lit by the weak moonlight, glimmered along the strands of the web, in which Someone had clearly spelled out: RAGNAROK.

That was the answer that had terrified me, all right.

The web reminded me of *Charlotte's Web*, a book my mother had read to Sage and me when we were small, and I couldn't help but giggle – even though the message here was more dire than the fate of a single pig.

The porch light snapped on, and Hilary came out onto the deck in her robe and slippers. "Webb? What are you doing out here? I thought I heard voices."

The robe, I noted, no longer closed all the way across her swelling belly. My brief amusement fled, as I pulled her into my arms and held on.

"Hey," she said tenderly, and kissed me. "Seriously, what's going on?"

"Where's Enkou?" I asked, only slightly tangentially.

She glanced at the pond. "I don't know. If he's not there, then he must be…" Then the spider web caught her eye, and her mouth dropped open.

"Yeah," I said.

She looked up at me, eyes wide. "It's starting all over again, isn't it?"

"Yeah."

She pillowed her head on my chest. "It never really ended, though, did it?"

In answer, I dropped my cheek to rest on top of her head. I hadn't realized until that moment how long we had both been waiting for the other shoe to drop. Our Earth had had peace for fifteen years – but peace always has a price.

We stood there for a long time, knowing it might be our last quiet moment. It was Hilary who pulled away. "I'll make coffee," she said.

"I'll call Mom," I said, and followed her inside to get my phone.

Before I dialed home, though, I hesitated. Instead, I went back out to the deck and took a photo of the web. The moon had nearly set, but the phone's flash did an adequate job of lighting up the message. I sent it to Mom, Dad, Sage, and Rafe, together with this message: "Had a visit from Iktomi."

I hadn't finished stirring milk into my first cup of coffee when Mom called. "Are you on your way up here?"

"Not yet. How soon do you want us?"

Exasperated, she replied, "Now!"

Even Hilary heard that. "You go ahead and get dressed," she said as I ended the call. "I'll tell the office I won't be in today."

"Let's hope it's just today," I muttered as I headed for our bedroom, although I had a pretty good idea of how crazy life was about to get.

# Chapter 2

We took Fossil – the ancient two-seat hovercar Mom had made Dad buy when they were brand-new to the market – and made it from Boulder to my parents' house in Golden in less than half an hour. It was still dark when we parked in front of the house. Every light on the first floor was ablaze, and Mom came out onto the porch to meet us.

The news I'd sent this morning seemed to have aged her overnight. Naomi Witherspoon had been thirty-five years old – she and Dad had just gotten married, and she hadn't changed her name yet – when she negotiated the power-sharing deal between Jehovah and the rest of the gods and goddesses. Now Mom was over seventy. Her hair, which had been long, straight, and black when I was a kid, was now short and white, and she had lost some of the matronly weight that she'd carried around for as long as I could remember. The kids at school used to tease me by calling her Naomi Battleship. Not to her face, of course; they weren't that stupid. And they wouldn't do it when Sage was around, either, because Sage's laser eyes would kick in, and then they'd have to explain to their mothers how their clothes got singed at school.

Anyway, Mom had always seemed stalwart to me. Now she seemed…bent. Hunched, even. It struck me for the first time that my parents were mortal, and that maybe Mom wasn't going to be up to this task. But if she couldn't do it, who could?

"There you are," she said, hugging each of us in turn. "Come on in. Dad's in the family room, and Uncle George and Aunt Shannon are on their way over."

"I should have texted Leonard," I said, whacking my forehead with the heel of one hand as we entered the house.

"I already took care of that," she said. "He's too busy to come down, but of course he's available if we need to consult with him." She closed the door behind us, and then paused. "Have you heard from your sister?"

"No."

Mom's expression didn't change, but she seemed to deflate a little more.

"She's probably on a mission, Mom."

"Sure," she said, her voice brittle. Things had not been going well between Mom and Sage for some time.

"I'll contact Captain Warren when we're done here," I said. Darrell Warren headed the quasi-governmental agency Sage and Rafe both worked for.

"No need," said Mom, back to her usual take-charge manner. "I'm sure your sister will check in when she's ready. Coffee?"

Dad was settled in his usual chair near the fireplace, but he rose to greet us. "Hi, Dad," Hilary said, and gave him a hug. He was in his mid-seventies, but looked younger than Mom; his hair was still salt-and-pepper and his carriage was spry. Sage and I had occasionally discussed whether it was good genetics or the gods that had kept Grandfather young for so long. We were pretty sure it was the gods. Now I wondered whether Coyote was slipping Dad an elixir on the sly – and if so, why White Buffalo Calf Pipe Woman wasn't doing the same for Mom.

We had just shed our coats and settled in with coffee when Uncle George and Aunt Shannon arrived, and the whole meet-and-greet process started all over again. Uncle George was still a bear of a man – not as tall as Dad, but broad-chested and sturdy. He clapped me on the back and asked me about some of the recent improvements I'd made to my studio. Aunt Shannon latched onto Hilary and began to grill her about her pregnancy; she was angling to be our midwife, as she had been for Mom when Sage and I were born, and Hilary was slowly coming around to the idea.

At last, we were all settled around the kitchen table with mugs of Mom's coffee and pastries from Woody Creek Bakery. It felt so homey and comfortable, even without Sage there, that I forgot for a moment that the world was about to come apart at the seams. I actually flinched when Mom said, "Tell us what Iktomi told you."

"Right. Sorry." I took another swig of coffee. "First, there was the dream."

"Iktomi came to you in a dream?" Dad asked.

"Let him tell it," said Mom, lightly tapping his forearm. "Go on, Webb."

"No, He didn't," I said to Dad, ignoring Mom. It was a fair question, after all. "The dream was about something different. But I'm sure they're connected." I went on to describe the hatchet-faced people outside their ice palaces, the familiar voice in my ear, and the monster made of smoke.

"Tell me again what Old Smoky said," Aunt Shannon urged. "Word for word, as much as you can remember."

Grinning a little, I said, "Y'know, I used to keep these revelations to myself so that I wouldn't have to suffer the third degree from you guys."

"And you could have done that this time, too," Aunt Shannon observed, "but you didn't. In fact, *you* brought it up. So tell me what he said."

I closed my eyes and thought back. "He knew me. He called me 'little web-maker.' And he said I knew him, although…" I shrugged, then went on to quote him: "'We have tangled before, and will do so again ere all is through. I have taken the measure of your talents, and found you wanting. This time, I shall prevail!'"

The old folks exchanged worried looks. "But you didn't recognize him," Dad said.

"Nope. There wasn't anything *to* recognize. He was all" – I cut a glance at Aunt Shannon and smirked – "smoky."

"And you said there was another voice?" Dad went on.

I leaned back and let my frustration show. "Yeah, and I wish I could place it. I know I've heard it before."

"Was it a god?" Mom asked.

"Maybe." I frowned. Even if it had been, that hardly narrowed it down.

"Did the speaker have an accent?" The gods could use or drop accents at will, but sometimes They forgot to play games with us.

"Not that I recall."

After a moment, Uncle George said, "Well, now. A dream could just be a dream, and we could chew this one over for days. But when a god actually shows up, you've got something. So tell us about what Iktomi said."

Again, I closed my eyes. "I was sitting on the deck and…meditating on the dream when He showed up," I said. I wasn't about to give *all* my secrets away. "He rose up from the shadows in the corner of the deck and told me that the agreement – the one Mom negotiated with the gods – was breaking down."

"I didn't negotiate with anybody," Mom said. "That's not how mediation works. But go on."

I gave her my best *okay, Mom* eye roll. "Anyway, He said, and I quote, 'It's going to be god against god before long, and Earth will be the final battleground.' He was about to say something else, I think, but He looked over His shoulder and…well…He kind of ordered me to tell you." She sat back at that, her brow furrowed with concern. "It wasn't until after He left that I noticed the spider web. It was almost like He couldn't tell me directly. Like Someone was preventing Him from speaking the word."

"Maybe it's not really Ragnarok," Aunt Shannon said. Everyone turned to her. "Well, the term has been shorthand for the end of the world when we've dealt with the gods before, hasn't it?"

"Shannon, honey, I love you, but that's not as comforting a thought as you meant it to be," said Uncle George.

"I didn't mean for it to be comforting," she returned tartly. "What I meant was that it might not be the Norse version of the end of the world. You know, with Baldur and Hodor coming back, and an attack from the Frost Giants, and all that stuff."

Hilary linked a hand around my elbow. "Could they have been Frost Giants in your dream?" she asked me.

I thought back to the hatchet-faced people and their icy homes, and shrugged. "Maybe. I've never seen a Frost Giant before, other than…" My head came up of its own accord. "Of course!"

"You've lost us, son," Dad said.

I looked around the table, making sure I had the attention of each pair of eyes. "It was Loki. The voice beside me in my dream belonged to Loki."

The older folks exchanged wide-eyed looks. "So," Aunt Shannon said in a small voice, "Iktomi really did mean Ragnarok. Terrific."

It made sense. Loki was half-Frost Giant, and the old stories placed Him at the head of a Frost Giant army when Ragnarok began. I'd thought it weird that the people in my dream were following me, but they might not have been; they might have been following Loki as He followed me, or caught up to me, or something.

Dad's thoughts had deviated onto a less benevolent track. Eyeing me, he said, "It wouldn't be the first time a couple of Tricksters have teamed up to cause trouble." He gave Mom a sidelong glance, and her mouth dropped open.

I caught the gist right away. "Hey, wait a minute," I protested. "I'm not going to help Loki. I hardly know the guy."

"You might not help Him directly," Dad said, "but Iktomi might."

*And since I'm allied with Iktomi…* "I'm still a free agent here," I argued.

Uncle George sided with me. "That's a pretty big leap you're making, Joseph. Besides, Iktomi didn't try to recruit Webb. All He did was tell him what's coming. I've never known a god yet who didn't just grab a human when He needed one."

"Or She," said Aunt Shannon.

"Or She," Uncle George amended. "And Iktomi might not be in league with Loki at all. Let's let this play out a little more, before you start consigning your son to eternity below a venom-dripping snake."

"I wasn't," Dad said. "I just want us to be prepared, that's all."

"Mom?" Hilary said, a note of concern in her voice.

We all looked at my mother. She had turned a little away from the rest of us and was staring at the fire, her elbow propped on the back of her dinette chair and her forehead in one hand. As if in response to Hilary's question, she turned to me and said, "Tell me everything you remember about the smoke creature."

"It seemed huge," I said. "It blotted out whatever the ambient light source was in my dream. At first I thought it was wearing the smoke like a cloaking device, but when it dissipated, I realized it *was* the smoke. There was nothing inside it at all." I shook my head. "And it was vicious. I got the sense that it enjoyed inflicting pain. That it got its jollies from it."

"There's no such thing as evil, Webb," Mom said sharply.

"I never said it was evil, did I?"

"No," said Aunt Shannon, "but that's what you're describing. A being that inflicts pain because it can, and because it enjoys the result."

"Was the thing in league with Loki, do you think?" Dad asked.

Uncle George rolled his eyes. "You've got a fixation on this concept of teamwork, bud."

Dad waved away his comment. "I'm trying to fill out my scorecard, that's all. If there's going to be a war, we need to know the players and which sides They're on."

"Scorecard," Uncle George scoffed. "This ain't March Madness, y'know. We're talking about the end of the world here."

"All the more reason to know who's working with whom."

While they bickered, I thought about Loki's reaction to the appearance of Old Smoky. "I don't think Loki reacted at all," I said to Mom. "I'm not even sure He was still there."

"Did He lead you to the smoke creature?"

"I don't think so. The crowd was following me, and Loki said in my ear, 'It begins.' And then the smoke thing showed up and I didn't notice anyone else but it. Him. Male voice."

"It was male? You're sure?" Mom said, sitting forward. When I nodded, she went on, "And Loki didn't say anything else?"

I shrugged helplessly and sat forward, my forearms resting on the table. "It was a dream, Mom. Scenes change quickly. You know that." Hilary put a hand on my arm, and I grabbed her hand and held on. "Why are you giving me the third degree, anyway? Why don't you contact White Buffalo Calf Pipe Woman and ask Her what's going on?"

"I've tried," she said, biting off each word precisely.

All of us stared at her. All except for Dad, who closed his eyes. Presumably he knew already.

She went on, with lawyerly detachment, "I've been trying. She hasn't been responsive."

In the silence that followed, Hilary said, "Maybe She's busy."

"More likely, She's being prevented from responding," Aunt Shannon said. "That would fit with the way Iktomi approached Webb – looking over His shoulder, and then disappearing before He was discovered talking to him."

"How long have you been trying, Mom?" I asked.

"About a week. Maybe a little longer." She glanced at Dad, who was now staring into his mug. "Your father has been having trouble contacting Coyote, too."

"Enkou," said Hilary, eyes wide.

I squeezed her hand. "When was the last time you saw him?"

"About a week ago, I think." She pushed her chair back and got to her feet. "I have to find him. He hates Loki for humiliating him that time." Loki had tricked Enkou into bowing so low that all the water poured out of the bowl-shaped depression on top of his head, rendering the little ninja turtle unable to move.

"Hang on, Hotaru," I said, catching her around the waist with one arm, using the name her Japanese-immigrant parents had given her at birth. "I'm sure Enkou's fine. He's pretty good at taking care of himself. But we'll look for him on the way home."

She gripped the edge of the table with both hands and nodded. "Okay. I'm just so worried about him."

Aunt Shannon smiled. "We know you are. We can all help you look in a little while. But right now, we need to spend a little more time figuring out what's going on. What about Benzaiten? Have you heard from Her?" The Shinto goddess of all that flows was Hilary's other divine protector. My sister had been beside herself when she learned that meek, quiet Hilary was allied with not just one god, but two.

"No," Hilary said now. "But that's not unusual. I'll go months at a time without hearing from Her."

Uncle George turned to Aunt Shannon, who shook her head. "Brighid's been laying low, too," she said.

"How can all of the gods be busy at once?" I asked.

"Everybody but Loki," said Dad, "who had time to contact you in a dream."

I looked around the table. Then I pulled out my phone and said to it, "Captain Warren."

"No, Webb," Mom said. "You might put your sister's job in jeopardy."

I glared at her. "We can't just sit around all day, playing what-if. We haven't got time. Maybe Darrell knows something." I broke off the staring contest with my mother when the phone line clicked.

"Captain Warren," the voice at the other end of the line boomed. "What's this about, Webb? We have something of a crisis on our hands."

"We may have more than something," I said, and put him on the holographic speaker. "I've got my mom and dad here, with my aunt and uncle, Shannon and George Lofton, and my girlfriend Hilary."

"Hey, everybody," Darrell said with a one-handed wave. His hologram manifested at the table as if he were seated between Mom and me.

"Where's my daughter?" Mom asked immediately, anxiety evident in her tone. "Is she all right?"

"She and Rafe are embedded, and their mission is at a delicate stage," he said. "I can't contact her, nor should you. But rest assured that I would know if there was a problem."

Mom nodded and looked away.

"Darrell," Dad asked, "have you spoken to Nanabush recently?"

That brought him up short. "No," he said at last.

"What about Morrigan?" Mom asked. "Has Tess seen Her?" Tess Showalter, one of the biggest names in the news business, was Darrell's wife.

Darrell looked at us as squarely as a hologram could. "No," he said again. "And the fact that you're asking these questions indicates to me that you know something's up. I'd appreciate it if you'd share with me what you know."

Everyone looked at me.

I debated, briefly, how much to share. The smoke being was the scariest of all the apparitions I had crossed paths with that night, but that threat seemed localized – aimed specifically at me. Before I let the government in on it, I wanted more time to puzzle it out for myself. So I said, "Loki showed up in my dream last night. He might have been leading an army of ice people. And when I woke up, Iktomi showed up on my back deck."

"Go on," Darrell said.

"He told me to tell my mother that the power-sharing agreement she'd mediated was falling apart, and that the war in heaven might spill over to Earth. His manner seemed furtive, and He appeared to be in a hurry to leave. And He left me this final message." I picked up the phone to send him the photo, but the signal wavered and we almost lost his hologram.

"I've got it," said Mom as she hit "send" on her own phone.

Darrell glanced at the photo, then back at us. "Iktomi's not wrong," he said. "I can't say much more because it has a bearing on the mission I've sent Sage and Rafe on. But thank you for telling me. Please keep me updated, and I promise to do the same for you." And his image blinked out.

Mom got up and braced her arms on the edge of the sink, staring out the window at nothing. Dad followed her and pulled her into an embrace.

"So what do we do?" asked Uncle George, breaking the silence.

Without letting go of my mother, Dad turned to regard him with a deadly serious gaze. "We figure out a way to get to the gods," he said. "If They won't come to us, we'll have to go to Them."

## The big sister speaks.

Good luck with all that, little brother.

As Webb said earlier, Rafe and I have been working for JAF-H/D – that's the U.S. Joint Assault Force, Hominid/Deific, to you civilians – for about a dozen years now. We're civilians ourselves, but we might as well be military for all the training we've received. We have to pass the Marine Corps' physical fitness tests, and we've been schooled in small weapons handling, CIA-style clandestine ops, and psychological warfare – just to name a few. Each of these would be a specialty in the regular armed forces, Darrell tells us, but we need to specialize in them all. "Don't think you can slack off here," he told us when we arrived, "just because you have a god or goddess backing you up. The gods may be gone someday, and if that day ever comes, the transition needs to be as seamless as possible. No gaps. No instability. Instability is an open invitation to all the lowlifes who have been skulking on the fringes, waiting to plunge the Earth back into the Dark Ages."

"You sound a little paranoid, sir," I'd said.

I'd meant it as a joke – I was still pretty cocky in those days – but Darrell fixed me with a look I'll never forget. "You *need* to be paranoid here, Sage," he said, his voice deadly calm. "Paranoia will help keep you alive."

Rafe and I exchanged a startled glance at that. But we'd only needed a couple of missions under our belts to find out he was right.

After twelve years of it, paranoia gets to be a way of life.

And it finally seemed like our training would pay off.

We had known for a while that something was up. Rafe, who's allied with Raven, hadn't seen his god in several weeks, and my own goddess, Cerridwen, had been missing in action as well.

But that wasn't our first clue. About a month before my family called my boss, Darrell's old Navy buddy Ducky – sorry, the Rev. Robert Duckworth of Palatine, Illinois – called to tell Darrell of an odd occurrence. Ducky is the rector of a liberal church in a liberal suburb of Chicago, and as such, he doesn't see much in the way of throwback behavior. But one day, one of his parishioners – a local businessman considered to be a fine, upstanding member of the community – told him in confidence that he was fighting the urge to beat his wife. Thoughts had begun plaguing him, the businessman said. Horrible, violent thoughts, about how women were put on this Earth to be subservient to man, and women who wouldn't submit should be physically punished. He swore he hadn't acted on these vile thoughts yet, but he was on the verge. Ducky said he recommended counseling, but the man wanted to pray with him. So Ducky and his parishioner sat down together and prayed – to Jehovah and to Jesus, with whom Ducky happens to be allied. And…nothing.

It wasn't a completely off-the-wall request; Jesus had sometimes been known to show up at Ducky's prayerful urging, when a parishioner was in particularly deep trouble. This was the sort of thing Jesus had responded to in the past. But this time, He didn't. And after nearly half an hour of continuous attempts to contact Him, the parishioner gave Ducky the sort of nasty grin that he hadn't seen in decades. The man then closed his business, laying off about fifty people, and he and his wife disappeared. Neither his former employees nor his erstwhile neighbors could tell Ducky anything – other than that the man had just recently started talking about taking a trip to the mountains of South Carolina. Why South Carolina specifically, nobody knew.

Darrell had a member of our team named Grady Stuart run a check on the man, whose name was Truro Barnstead, and his wife Agnes. Grady is nearly as good with computerized searching as Hilary – or as Webb, for that matter. Anyway, Grady found vehicle registration info immediately, and Darrell had the cops put out an APB on the car. The trail ran cold just across the Ohio River in Kentucky. I was convinced we'd find the car ditched in some backwater town, with a corresponding report of a stolen car or bus tickets or something. But no – a day later, the vehicle turned up abandoned at a state park in Oconee County, South Carolina, west of Greenville. Local police had heard reports of a fundamentalist group that was hiding out up in the mountains, but they didn't know much beyond that. Or didn't want to tell us more, anyway.

"Maybe the fundies are buying off the cops," Grady speculated.

"Maybe the fundies recruited the cops," Rafe said.

"Or maybe they've threatened the cops' wives and families," I said.

"Or maybe they're all kin to these good ol' boys," said Grady, laying his Carolina accent on thick. "I don't know if y'all know it? But mountain folk can be sweet as Moon Pie to outsiders, all while they're closing up ranks so you cain't see a durn thing behind 'em."

"Yeah, we know it," said Rafe with a grin aimed at me. I knew what the grin was for; we knew somebody who had a Carolina accent nearly as thick as Grady's fake one: Hilary Takahashi, my former college roommate who had gotten herself knocked up by my little brother. Rafe's smile faded a bit as he said, "You know, Sage…"

"No."

"It's one phone call to Hilary. You wouldn't have to talk to your mother."

"I said *no*, Rafe. I have nothing to say to any of them."

"You know," he said, "you've never given your mother a chance to tell you her side of it."

I stared him down. "Let's. Not. Do. This. Right. Now."

"Do what?" asked Darrell as he entered our situation room.

"Nothing." I glared at Rafe for good measure and faced my computer screen, turning my back on the men – as much to hide my reddened face as anything else. Sometimes I still couldn't figure out why I'd married Rafe.

After a brief pause, Darrell cleared his throat. "Well, whatever that was about, you two lovebirds will have to patch it up fast. I'm sending you on a mission."

"Where to?" Rafe asked, sounding almost eager.

"Oconee County, South Carolina," said Darrell. "Your job is to infiltrate the fundamentalist group that sucked the Barnsteads in, and figure out what's going on there."

I spun in my chair, incredulous. "You want me to let him dominate me?" I said, hooking a thumb at Rafe.

"Yes," was all Darrell said.

"Good luck with that," said Grady.

I had to agree. But a mission was a mission. I prepared to suck it up and pretend to be subservient for as long as it took.

Too bad I didn't think to swap places with Webb. Then I would have been trying to infiltrate the gods' hideout instead of the project Darrell had proposed. And I wouldn't have had to pretend to be anyone but me.

## Chapter 3

The trouble was that we didn't know how to get to the gods' parallel universe, if you will, without having one of the gods take us there. We knew of several portals into Their world, the closest being the one near Boulder where Grandfather's wickiup used to be. But that one had been sealed off twice: first, when Pele sealed the passages with molten lava as my parents escaped from the Mexica mother goddess Coatlicue; and second, when the gods converted the place into a giant chamber for processing carbon dioxide out of the atmosphere so that life on Earth wouldn't either fry or drown (your choice) – a use to which the chamber was still being put.

My family's history with the gods has been somewhat complex.

Anyway, the next closest portal that I knew of was in Alaska, and it opened into the Slavic underworld, beneath the roots of the World Tree. We'd have a long, hard climb up the trunk of that thing to get to the home of the Slavic pantheon. And none of us knew whether the war was even going on there – it might be limited to the Norse neighborhood. Assuming such a concept as neighborhoods existed among the gods. Even after all these years, there was still so much we didn't know about Them. We'd pretty much always let Them come to us.

"We need a shaman," Dad said. The sun had long since been up. We were on our third pot of coffee and had just discussed whether to order Mexican food for lunch, yet we were no closer to figuring out how to get into the gods' world.

"Didn't you say you had called Leonard?" I asked Mom. Leonard was her cousin, and a Wolf Dreamer among the Lakota.

She nodded. "No reply so far."

"Not surprising, I guess. He's often out," I said. Leonard spent a lot of time roaming the Badlands, seeking answers to his people's problems through visions. Surely, though, if he'd had one that involved what we were currently discussing, he would have contacted us. "What about Rafe's mother?" Sandy Hanlon was Tlingit, and had once become Bear Mother before my eyes.

"It would take too long – and be too expensive – to get all of us to their portal," Dad said.

"Well, yeah. But we don't need to hop a plane to Alaska in order to get hold of her," I said. "We could just call."

Mom was already reaching for her phone. "Hello, Sandy?" she said, and then stopped, frustration writ large on her face. She held up the phone so we could hear the voicemail message: *Please leave your name and number…* She did, and ended the call. "Anyone else?"

"Kurt Lange," said Dad.

Mom whacked her forehead and began searching her contacts for the number. Kurt was allied with Thor. Or *was* Thor – I was never clear on that point. In any case, Kurt ought to know what was going on. "All I've got for him is a work number," Mom said, and tried it. "Hello, this is Naomi Curtis. Is Mr. Lange available?…Oh. I see…And you don't have any idea how to contact him?…I see. Well, thank you. I'll try to contact him another way."

"Well?" Aunt Shannon said impatiently as Mom ended the call.

"He retired several years ago, without leaving any forwarding information." She sighed. "I guess he figured there was no point. Even overnight shipping services won't deliver to the gods' realm." She looked pointedly at Dad, who was wearing a pained expression. "What?"

"I have another idea, but you're not going to like it," he said.

"How do you know?"

"Because I hate it. But it might work."

"Let's hear it."

But he didn't say anything; instead, he seemed to be trying to flash her a message with her eyes. At last, she got it, and the corners of her mouth drew down in distaste. "Damn it. You're right, but…damn it." She turned to the rest of us and said, "Okay, everybody. Field trip."

"Where are we going?" Aunt Shannon asked as we got to our feet.

"Governor's Park. To pay a visit to our local former President."

"Oh, gods," said Aunt Shannon, her nose wrinkling in distaste. "Couldn't we just call? Antonia would talk to us."

"If we can get through the layers of voice mail," I said. "I think Mom's right. Better to show up on their doorstep."

"If we can get through the security cordon," she said. "Why didn't the gods get rid of automated receptionists, anyway?"

"Are you kidding?" said Dad. "It's a perfect system for Someone who never, ever wants to talk to a human."

I looked at Hilary. "Coming with us, Hotaru?" I asked, slipping an arm around her shoulders. I'd been noticing her fidgeting next to me, the longer we sat.

She leaned into me. "I think I'll just stay here. Maybe take a walk."

"Good idea," Aunt Shannon said with an approving nod. She didn't fill in the blank, but I knew what she was going to say: Pregnant women need to get lots of exercise. So I smiled at her, even though I knew Hilary well enough to know what she was actually thinking: She wasn't inclined to spend a couple of hours in the car on what could prove to be a fruitless errand, when she could walk along the creek in my parents' patch of woods and try to contact Enkou.

I bent over and kissed Hilary. "*Ganbatte*," I whispered in her ear.

"*Domo*," she whispered back. "Keep me posted. I'll have my phone."

Even without Hilary, it was a tight fit in Mom's urban assault vehicle. Dad rode shotgun, with Uncle George and me taking the window spots in the back seat and Aunt Shannon sandwiched between us. It wasn't a small vehicle, but neither Uncle George nor I were small men.

Mom glanced in the rear-view mirror at us. "Joseph, trade places with your son," she said.

"I'm fine, Naomi," said Aunt Shannon. "Just drive, okay?"

"Okay," Mom said in resignation, and hooked her right arm over her seat back so she could back up the car. Her mouth was set in a determined line – too determined, I thought, for the business at hand. I exchanged wondering frowns with Aunt Shannon. Clearly she didn't know what was going on with my mother, either.

I closed my eyes for a moment and immersed myself in the timestream. I figured whatever was going on with Mom ought to be pretty easy to track.

I found the channel I wanted, all right, but I couldn't grab hold of the stream. No matter what I did to try to snag it, the bright beam of light eluded me. I lifted myself out of the channel and hovered, centering myself, before going off to chase the timestream I'd found and abandoned that morning: the one that would unravel the mystery surrounding Iktomi's message to me. Presently, I found that one, too, and dipped down to find the light path again, as I had earlier in the day. But now this path, too, refused my grip.

I rose above the stream again. It wasn't the first time this sort of thing had happened. Far from it, in fact. Usually it meant that I was going to be involved somehow – but how I could be involved in both the gods' war and whatever my mother was going through, I had no idea.

I glanced down the timestream to see whether the two events intersected or joined at some future point. Once in a while, I'd been able to see the blockage – although not what caused it or how it was solved – and jump into the stream past the problem area to see how events panned out in the end. Such blockages would look like a tangle of light – as if a cat had gotten hold of a ball of yarn and made a knot that would take hours to unravel. In this case, though, I couldn't see a problem. In fact, I couldn't see anything. Past a certain point, the entire timestream was obscured by a dark gray mist. Like fog. Or smoke.

My dream of the smoke being had been too recent. I backpedaled in a hurry and rose back up to *now*, shuddering.

Aunt Shannon felt my trembling, of course, and eyed me with much the same look she'd given Mom a few minutes earlier. I offered her a weak grin and a shrug, which I don't think she bought.

Still, she turned away and glanced past Uncle George, out the window. Thirty seconds later, she said, "Hey, what's up with that guy? Naomi, do you see him?"

"Looks like he's…panhandling? What the hell?" Mom pulled over immediately, earning a honk from the driver behind her. She responded with a cheerful wave as Aunt Shannon and Uncle George piled out of the car.

"I'm just going to ask him…" Aunt Shannon said.

"I know what you're going to ask him," said Uncle George as they started back toward the man on the sidewalk. "That's why I'm going with you."

"What's a panhandler?" I asked my parents.

Mom and Dad shared a look before Dad replied. "Back before the Second Coming, governments weren't always all that supportive of poor people. Some of the people in charge didn't want their money going to support people who didn't have any of their own."

"But that's cruel," I said.

"And greedy," said Mom. "And stupid and short-sighted, because anyone could find themselves in need of help at any time. Money can't solve every problem, no matter how much of it you hoard." She shook her head. "Anyway, go on, Joseph."

"These short-sighted idiots expected the churches to provide for all the poor people," Dad said. "But some churches didn't see that as their mission. Some took it on, but required the people they were helping to hear a sermon first. And some pastors thought they needed the money worse than the poor did, so they'd skim off the top for themselves."

"Sometimes they'd do more than skim," Mom added.

"It sounds horrible," I said.

"It was," Dad said. "Poor people took to sitting on street corners with signs asking for money. Some of them were con artists, but often people really needed the money. Either way, they were called beggars or panhandlers."

I looked back at the man with the sign. Uncle George and Aunt Shannon were deep in discussion with him. A minute later, Aunt Shannon put her hand on the panhandler's shoulder – a comforting gesture that should not have rocked the man the way it did, except that Aunt Shannon was a healer trained by the Irish goddess Brighid Herself. The man reared back in surprise, blinking up at her. As he got to his feet, Uncle George pulled out his wallet and handed him some money. Then they said goodbye and ambled back to the car.

"Brock needs to hear about this," was the first thing Aunt Shannon said when she got back in the car.

"Oh, he will," said Mom as she pulled out into traffic again. "Trust me."

I was still wrapping my brain around the idea of panhandling. I could not conceive of a world in which the unfortunate were not taken care of. "What just happened?" I asked.

"The guy was panhandling," Uncle George said, his voice rising in outrage on the final word.

I squeezed my eyes shut. "I got that part," I said, "and Dad explained the concept. I guess what I'm asking is how it could have happened at all."

Aunt Shannon took a deep breath to try to calm herself, but I could still feel the anger radiating from her in waves. "The man said he'd had a job and a girlfriend just three or four months ago, but then the bottom fell out of his life. Couldn't get out of bed. Didn't see the point."

"He was depressed?" I asked.

"Why didn't he get help?" Mom said at the same time.

Aunt Shannon's response served us both. "It didn't occur to him, I guess. He said it was like a black cloud had descended on him." Her eyes met mine, and I shuddered again. How long had the smoke being been planning this?

"So you broke through the smoke by touching him," I said.

She rocked a hand in a seesaw motion. "There was a little more to it than that, but essentially, yes."

"Did you" – I swallowed – "did you sense anything behind the smoke?"

"You mean, did I sense a malevolent being like the one in your dream? No. The thing must have cursed and run."

"But why now?" Mom asked.

"Good question," Uncle George rumbled. "Let's ask Brock that, too."

Dad locked gazes with him for a moment. Then he stared out the windshield.

The subtext here – which everyone in the car knew, but you may not, unless you've read my mother's books – is that my mother dated former President Brock Holt for years before she met my father. They were even engaged briefly, until Mom realized Brock was in league with Loki. And while Dad came to tolerate Loki for a while, and even saw Him as an ally on occasion, he never warmed up to President Holt. The President, being a politician, had learned to be gracious to my father – especially after he married Antonia Greco, who at the time was the host of a highly-rated news magazine on NWNN.

Anyway, the Holts maintained their rambling faux-Victorian in Denver's Governor's Park neighborhood while he was in office, and after he finished his two terms and retired from public office, they moved back. President Holt dabbled in an assortment of environmental causes, but Mom thought it was mainly because it allowed him to go skiing whenever he wanted. Snarky as her comment was, it might have been true; the President had suffered a compound leg fracture on the slopes in his 60s, and ever since then, he and his wife spent the majority of their time in Denver. Antonia had quit working in TV when she became First Lady, and never seemed interested in going back into the news business after they left Washington.

Despite the improvements the gods had made to life on Earth, the U.S. government had never been comfortable with the idea of doing away with the Secret Service. Just because the gods punished swiftly, it didn't mean some yahoo would never think to try something. So the Holts had a security cordon around their home that rivaled the one they'd had in Washington. Two people in black trench coats and sunglasses manned the front gate, and one waved us to a stop while the other spoke into a microphone clipped to her shoulder.

Mom rolled down her window and smiled brightly at the agent. "Hi," she said. "I'm Naomi Curtis. We're all friends of the Holts. Would you please let Antonia know we're here?"

The man glanced over the hood of our car to the woman in the gatehouse. She shook her head, and the man turned back to Mom. "I'm sorry, ma'am, but your license tag is not on the list of approved vendors."

"Vendors?" Uncle George roared. "Didn't you hear the lady? Don't you know who she *is*?"

"Don't hassle the Secret Service guy, George," Dad said.

"I'm sorry, ma'am," the agent said again, "but I'm going to need to see IDs for everyone in the car."

Tight-lipped, Mom began fishing in her bag.

"This is horseshit," Aunt Shannon said under her breath as she tapped something into her phone. Then she collected driver's licenses from her husband and me, and handed them to Mom to give to the agent.

"Thank you. Please wait here," the man said, deadpan. Then he walked back to the booth, where the woman agent was still chatting with whoever was at the other end of her microphone.

"As if we had a choice," Mom said.

Aunt Shannon's phone burbled. She glanced at it and grinned. "We're in," she said.

Mom turned in her seat. "What did you do?"

Still grinning, Aunt Shannon nodded toward the gatehouse, where an old-fashioned phone on the wall was ringing insistently. The woman agent broke off her conversation long enough to lift the handset from the wall, wince at the barrage of words coming out of the earpiece, and replace the handset. She nodded in chagrin to her fellow agent, who sprinted back to our car. "Sorry for the confusion, Ms. Curtis, Mr. Curtis," he said, nearly fumbling our IDs in his haste to get them back to us. "Of course, you're welcome any time. Please drive through."

The gate was already swinging open to admit us. Mom inclined her head graciously as she handed the cards to Dad to redistribute, then sailed us serenely through the gate.

Only then did Aunt Shannon show me her phone. Two texts were on display:

**Shannon:** We're at your gate and the SS won't let us in
**Antonia:** Assholes! Hang on...

"Nice," I said approvingly. "The 'SS' part was a particularly deft touch."

"Thanks," she said. "I was pretty proud of it, myself."

Uncle George peered at the screen. "Now is that any way for a nice old lady to talk?"

"Hey, Antonia's the one who called them assholes," she said. "And anyway, who said I was nice?"

In response, he kissed her.

"Keep it clean, you two," Dad said as we pulled up to the front door.

The agents here were all deferential, opening doors for us and nodding politely as if nothing untoward had happened at the gate. In their view, probably, nothing had.

Antonia met us in the foyer. "Thank the gods you're here!" she said, embracing each of us in turn. "I've been trying to figure out how to get hold of you."

"You could have picked up the phone," Naomi said.

Antonia opened her mouth to reply, then seemed to think better of it. "Come on in. Have you had lunch? I was just about to sit down."

"That sounds awesome," I said, before somebody could demur. Breakfast had been hours before, and we'd never gotten around to ordering lunch.

"Come on in," she said, and led us through a couple of well-appointed rooms to a large and even more well-appointed dining room. A Federal-style table that looked as if it might support several leaves dominated the room, with probably twenty chairs lining the walls, and hutches in opposite corners displaying the Holts' Presidential china. I knew from previous visits that they had left the government-owned set behind in Washington, but Antonia had paid for a duplicate set for their own house. The room had an 18th-century Americana feel, but the paintings on the walls depicted Colorado scenes, and a Navajo rug – Teec Nos Pos style, I thought, judging by the bright colors and the intricate diamond-and-triangle central design – lay on the floor under the table.

Antonia told us to have a seat while she informed the cook that she needed to whip up a few more servings. When she returned and took her own seat, Mom asked, "So where's Brock?"

"He's not here," Antonia said.

"I noticed. Where is he?"

"On a business trip. So how have you all been? It's been ages since we've seen you."

I'm no master at reading people, but even I could tell she was being evasive – and I could also tell Mom didn't approve. "Antonia, we didn't come here with no notice to exchange pleasantries. We need to talk to Brock," she said.

"He's not here," Antonia said again, and this time I caught a note of desperation in her voice. "Please, let's have lunch. Then we can chat. We do have a lot to catch up on." As she spoke, she cast her eyes pointedly toward the ceiling – and now I spotted the security camera nestled into the chandelier.

"Shut up, Mom, I'm starving," I said, doing my best to sound like a bored teenager.

Mom scowled, but Antonia flashed me a grateful grin. The soup and salad arrived just then, and we all made the appropriate noises while we ate. That was followed by sandwiches, and brownies for dessert.

"Why don't you ever make brownies, Naomi?" Dad said as he helped himself to a second one.

"Antonia has a cook," Mom pointed out.

He shrugged. "We could have a cook, too."

"I don't want a cook," Mom said.

"But then we could have brownies every day."

Mom put down her brownie and looked at him. "Our kitchen is fully functional. If you want brownies every day, you could make them yourself."

"But that's not the same as *having* brownies every day," I chimed in.

"See? Webb understands what I'm talking about," said Dad. "Thank you, son."

"Come on, Joseph," said Aunt Shannon. "You knew Naomi was no culinary artist when you married her."

"She *pushed* me," he said, grinning.

"I did not!"

*Pushing*, you see, is Mom's most useful magical power. White Buffalo Calf Pipe Woman gave it to her before She told her what it was for: to force the gods to come together and figure out how to make things better on Earth. That lack of information was how Mom ended up engaged to President Holt; she *pushed* him to propose without realizing what she was doing.

Her other magical power involves glowing with an argent fire when she experiences righteous anger – which scared the crap out of Sage and me when we were kids, let me tell you.

"Done?" Antonia asked brightly, and cleared the plates herself. Then she closed all the doors and flipped a switch behind a recessed panel in the wall near the kitchen door. Only then did she let her guard down. Fear and exhaustion were plain on her face as she told us, "Brock's not on a business trip. He's gone, and so is Loki."

"What about Diana?" Mom asked. Antonia was pledged to the Greek goddess of the hunt.

She raised her hands in frustration. "I can't get hold of Her. I don't know what's going *on*, Naomi, and it's killing me."

"When did you last see Brock?" Dad asked.

"Last night. He went to bed early because his leg was bothering him. When I went up to go to bed myself, the lights were on and the TV was blaring, but Brock had fallen asleep. I turned everything off and went to sleep myself. This morning…" She paused and wiped her eyes with the heel of one hand. Aunt Shannon handed her a tissue.

"You're sure he didn't just leave?" Uncle George asked.

"That was the first thing I thought of. But his suitcase and briefcase are still where he left them when he got home from his most recent trip. His schedule doesn't show anything. His clothes and his cell phone are still here. And he hasn't been acting weird, like he needed to get away or anything."

"What do you think happened?" Mom asked.

Antonia blew out a breath. "I think Loki's taken him somewhere."

"And what makes you think that?"

"Because He's been acting strange for the past week or so, popping in to talk to Brock at odd hours and so on. He didn't share any of His plans with Diana – I know that much, at least."

The discussion went on along these same lines for a while, but I was distracted by a corner of the Navajo rug at my feet. The Navajo are known for their stunningly beautiful weavings, but no matter what design the weaver uses, he or she always includes a lifeline – a line of color from the main section of the rug that extends through the border to the rug's edge. The lifeline is there to give anyone, weaver or viewer, a way out, in case they get too wrapped up in the complexity of the design.

In this instance, it appeared to me that a spider was crawling along the edge of the rug, weaving in a brand-new lifeline.

"Webb?" Mom said, and my head snapped up. "Didn't you hear me? I asked you to tell Antonia about your dream."

So for the second or third time that day – I was beginning to lose track – I explained again about the possible Frost Giants, Loki's voice, and the smoke being.

"And we saw a very strange thing on our way here," Aunt Shannon said when I had finished, and began explaining about the panhandler we'd seen on our way over.

I glanced back down at the rug, but the spider and the new lifeline were gone – if they had ever existed at all.

I was suddenly overcome with exhaustion. There were too many weird things happening, too many details I was missing amidst all this talking. And I'd had too little sleep.

Then it dawned on me that Loki had contacted me after he'd spirited the President away. And I'd left Hilary alone at Mom's house.

"Excuse me," I said, standing abruptly. "I need to check on something." And I hurried out, ignoring Mom calling after me.

I'd noticed a door to the backyard in one of the rooms we had traveled through on our way in. I backtracked until I found it, and let myself outside. Then I called Hilary.

"Hey," she said in her Southern accent, and I began to breathe freely again. "Where are you?"

"At the Holts'," I told her.

"Whoo hoo," she said. "Rubbin' elbows with the bigwigs."

"I'd rather be rubbing other things with you," I said.

"Whoo hoo," she said, in a completely different tone. "How much longer are you gonna be?"

"I don't know. Mom's calling the shots." I leaned against the side of the house and blew out a breath, watching it fog the air. "Stuff's going down all over, Hotaru. Did you have any luck with Enkou?"

"No," she said. "I want to go home. I'm sure he's there. I never had a chance to check the creek this morning."

I was just as sure that we wouldn't find him at Boulder Creek, or anywhere else on this plane of existence. "I'll see if I can shake Mom loose."

"Use me as an excuse, if you have to. Say I thought I was in premature labor or something."

"And get Aunt Shannon all wound up? No way. Then we'll never get home."

She chuckled. "You're right, I guess. I'll leave it to your judgment."

We both got sappy for a few seconds, and then I ended the call. When at last I looked up, I noticed Dad hovering on the other side of the door. "Your mother sent me," he said as I came in. "Everything okay?"

"Everything's fine," I confirmed, "except no Enkou yet. And Hilary's asking when we'll be back. She wants to go home."

"Can't blame her," Dad said. "So do I. But your mom's in the middle of cooking up a TV interview with Tess Showalter."

"Can't she do that at home?"

"Let's go ask her," Dad said, and led the way back to the dining room.

We stopped just inside the door. Antonia was pacing while Mom chatted with Tess by speaker phone. Mom glanced up at us; Dad hooked a thumb toward the door, and she ended the call with a *we'll talk later*. Then she gave Antonia a long hug.

"I'm so glad you came over," Antonia said into Mom's shoulder.

"Everything is going to work out fine," Mom said. "We'll get to the bottom of this and get Brock back in no time."

"Let me see you out," Antonia said.

"Don't bother," Mom said with a smile and a wave. "We know the way." And we all trooped toward the front door.

When we were out of earshot of the dining room, Mom asked me, "Is Hilary okay?"

"Yeah, fine," I said. "But she wants to go home to look for Enkou."

"She won't find him." Mom cut a glance at me.

I looked away. "Yeah, I know."

Aunt Shannon patted my shoulder as Dad asked, "So what's the plan?"

Mom blew out a breath. "I'm going to do a live shot with Tess tomorrow where we lay it all out: Brock's missing, the gods are unreachable, and we think something dire is happening."

"You're not going to mention Ragnarok specifically, are you?" I asked.

"Not if I can help it," Mom said. "But we've got to do something to get the gods' attention. They can't shut us out forever."

"Not without saying goodbye," Aunt Shannon said softly. She and Brighid had been very close.

I gripped her shoulder in return. That's when I noticed, perched on the cuff of my jacket, a spider. I was sure it was the same one I'd seen on the Holts' dining room rug – especially when it reared up and waved its front legs at me. *Iktomi?* But when I blinked, it was gone.

I sighed. It looked like things were going to get a whole lot weirder before it was all over.

# Chapter 4

Mom handed me the keys, which was so uncharacteristic of her that eyebrows were raised all around. She ignored us all, though, as she made to sit in back with Dad and Aunt Shannon, leaving Uncle George to ride shotgun. As Dad helped Mom into the car, Uncle George leaned toward me. "What's going on with your mother?"

"I wish I knew. She hasn't said anything to Aunt Shannon, then?"

"Hell, no. If she had, I wouldn't be asking you."

I glanced in the rear-view mirror to see whether everybody was seated – which is how I saw Aunt Shannon grab Mom's hand for support, and the look of shock on her face as their hands connected. "Naomi?" she said.

"Not now," Mom said crossly. Situated at last, she leaned against Dad and said, "Tess wanted me to fly to Washington for the interview, but I told her to forget it. So she and her crew are taking the shuttle to Denver instead." She glanced at Dad. "Antonia wants to do it at her house. I guess they have a room that's already set up for that sort of thing."

"A broadcast studio?" I said. She nodded. "Makes sense. I'm sure it was installed during their time in the White House."

"Probably." She leaned against Dad's shoulder and closed her eyes. "I tried to get them to come to our house, but Antonia said no way. So I'll need a ride."

"Why can't you drive yourself?" I asked, glancing at my parents in the rear-view mirror. Dad frowned at me and shook his head slightly. I knew *he* wasn't going to take her; for as long as I could remember, he had avoided driving with others in the car, in case Coyote took control of him without warning. It had happened less and less frequently as the years passed, and seemed more unlikely now than ever, given the gods' pointed absence. But I was sure Dad would still consider the precaution worthwhile.

"I'll take you," Aunt Shannon offered.

But Mom said, "Webb can do it."

I tried very hard not to roll my eyes. "Mom, I have my own life. In Boulder. Where I need to finish a project proposal by next Wednesday. And where Hilary has a job that she kind of needs to keep."

"It's important to your mother," Dad put in.

What the heck? Dad was taking Mom's side? "Fine," I said, gritting my teeth. "I'll run Hilary home and be back in the morning. What time is the interview?"

"Tess is arriving on the 8:00 a.m. shuttle," said Mom. "I figure she's aiming for the noon Eastern time show, which is ten our time. But we'll all need to prep before we go on the air. So we should leave the house at eight."

"Nobody goes 'on the air' any more, Mom," I said. I couldn't resist a dig, given the assignment she'd just given me. "No cable, either – everything's done through the Internet now."

She waved a hand at me and closed her eyes again. "You knew what I meant."

I sighed. "Fine. I'll be there at 7:30."

Breaking the news to Hilary was another matter. "Well, *that's* inconvenient. Why can't she drive herself?"

"Good question," I said. I hadn't had a chance to talk to Aunt Shannon; when we got back home, they hopped out of Mom's car and straight into theirs. "There's something weird going on with her."

"She always has something weird going on with her," Hilary said – uncharacteristically cranky for her. But then she'd called in sick to work, only to spend the day cooling her heels in Golden while my family borrowed me for unspecified Important Things.

"Look, I'm not crazy about any of this, either," I said. "I've still got that grant proposal to finish, and the deadline is a week from now. But instead of working on it tomorrow, I'm going to have to drive Mom around town again." I took a breath, trying to get a handle on my frustration. Going off on Hilary wasn't going to solve anything. "I do think something weird is going on, though. You know how Aunt Shannon can tell by touch if someone is sick?"

"Yeah, I know. Ever since we told her I was pregnant, she's got to hold my hand every time she sees me." Her hand strayed to her belly. "It's creepy."

"Well, it is, but that's just Aunt Shannon," I said. "Anyway, she grabbed Mom's hand to help her into the car this afternoon, and her eyes got really wide. *Really* wide."

"You think she's sick?"

That was exactly what I thought, but I had this superstitious fear that voicing the words would make them true. Instead, I nodded.

"Aunt Shannon could cure her, though, couldn't she?"

"It's in her toolbox, for sure," I said. "But there have been a few times when she hasn't been able to." Aunt Shannon was superb at delivering babies, or so I'd been told. But she didn't have a medical degree – she had trained as a therapist, not a psychologist – and she was better at curing magical ills than the regular kind.

"But she'll try, right?"

"As long as Mom will let her. And I'm not convinced she will."

Hilary shook her head. "Seems silly to me, but okay. Anyhow, you don't need me tomorrow, do you?"

"Baby, you know I need you every day," I said, pitching my voice low and sexy.

She giggled. "You know what I meant. To come along on the drive. I need to go back to work."

"Yeah, no, that should be fine."

She nodded, distracted. We were almost home, and she was scanning the side of the road. "Can we stop at the creek?"

"That was the plan," I said, taking the left to go behind the university fieldhouse.

The first time I'd been to Enkou's creekside hidey-hole, he had informed me in broken English that I was acceptable as an escort for Hilary. The kappa's English had improved somewhat over the intervening fifteen years, and he still liked me most of the time. We made an odd little family: Hilary, her kappa, and me. I occasionally wondered how Enkou would react to the baby's arrival – whether he would disappear in a jealous snit or, worse, plot tricks to play on our helpless infant. He had never seemed like a mean-spirited Trickster – unlike, say, Loki. But sometimes pranks are funnier in the imagination than in their execution. I'd had my share of personal experience with the phenomenon.

Hilary stepped up her pace as we approached the creek, singing out, "Enkou-san!"

As I followed more sedately, I glanced at the sky above the Flatirons. Clouds had begun to gather, and they looked like they might bring us snow. It shouldn't have surprised me – it was October, after all, and the higher elevations can get snow in August – but I wasn't mentally prepared for winter yet. Maybe because the baby was due in mid-December, and I wasn't yet ready to take on my socially-approved role as Family Breadwinner. The grant, if I got it, was substantial enough so that I would finally be able to say I was supporting my family – if only until the award ran out. But by then I'd have a reputation, or so I hoped, and financial support for my work might come more easily after that.

The gods were supposed to have taken care of this. One of the things They claimed to support at the outset was capital-A Art – the creation of all things inventive, if not necessarily beautiful. Artists weren't supposed to live in poverty any more. They – we – weren't supposed to have to suffer for our art. But somehow, those good intentions got shoved aside, what with all the more pressing problems that needed to be fixed first.

And now the gods were gone – off to battle each other, if Iktomi's message was to be believed – and arts funding might never get the attention it deserved.

Had it really been only that morning that I'd seen the message on the deck? It seemed like days had elapsed since then.

"Enkou-san!" Hilary called again, breaking me out of my reverie. I crossed my arms against a newly-perceived chill and followed the sound of her voice.

"He's not here," she said as soon as I joined her. "I was so sure he'd be here." She hid her face in my jacket as I wrapped my arms around her and scanned the creekside myself. I could see where Enkou typically burrowed himself into the bank – there was definitely a kappa-sized hole between the boulders – but it was empty.

"Let's go home," I told Hilary. "Maybe he's waiting for us there."

But I knew he wouldn't be. And he wasn't.

"He's just gone," she said. "Just like the others."

It occurred to me then that my beloved girlfriend had never been without her little buddy. People in my parents' generation who had personal relationships with the gods had been in their twenties and thirties when those relationships began. Well, my father was a special case – he'd been channeling Coyote since his teens, or maybe even earlier. But Mom had been Sage's age, more or less, when White Buffalo Calf Pipe Woman had contacted her the first time.

The kids in my generation had had gods as their lifelong companions. I didn't know when Rafe was first aware of Raven, but Sage had been allied with Thunderbird since birth. Granted, neither Thunderbird nor Iktomi were the kind of touchy-feely deity you wanted to invite to your birthday party, so maybe Sage and I weren't feeling the lack as acutely as Hilary obviously was.

The gods had left us the powers They'd granted us, but we couldn't count on Them any more. It almost felt like someone had died.

Hilary went about the process of pulling together dinner for the two of us, but her heart wasn't in it. She picked at the food on her plate, then declared herself too tired to eat and turned in. I wanted nothing more than to join her – my sleep had been interrupted earlier than hers had – but I needed to work on that grant application.

So instead of toddling off to beddy-bye, I went into my studio and fired up the computer.

The mock-up was done; I just needed to use the 3D printer to make it, and knit the fluttery bits that would then be affixed to the pinnacles. The final product would be seven feet tall and twenty feet wide, but the mock-up was small enough to fit in a banker's box. It was the application form that was giving me trouble. I was usually creative enough to bluff my way through these types of things, but a lot was riding on this application. A *lot*. Basically, my whole professional life.

I sat down at my desk and opened the application. This, too, was nearly done. I was stymied by just one question: *In the committee's view, art should have a lasting impact on society as a whole. What lasting societal impact do you envision for your installation?*

I sat back and rubbed my eyes. Honestly? Not a whole lot.

What I wanted to say was that I came from a line of people who do extraordinary things all the time. My mother and father had facilitated the agreement between the gods and goddesses that brought about the Second Coming. My sister and her husband had convinced the gods to help us reverse climate change and save the Earth; my girlfriend had run the numbers for them. My aunt-by-association had a magical healing ability. My cousin Leonard was a trusted adviser to his people.

Me? I play with yarn.

*What lasting societal impact…*

I propped my chin on my hand and stared at the screen. In seconds, I was asleep.

The first word out of my mouth, as Hilary shook me awake the next morning, was, "Crap." I knew as soon as I saw where I was that I'd screwed up.

"You needed the sleep," she said, handing me a cup of coffee. She was already dressed for work, in a shirt with drapey sleeves over skinny pants. She wore high-heeled ankle boots and had her long, dark hair twisted into a bun at the nape of her neck.

"Thanks, babe." I wrapped my hands around the mug gratefully. Then I glared at the computer screen, which had sprung to life as soon as I bumped the mouse. "I just don't know what to put for this last question. *Lasting societal impact* is what Mom and Dad and Sage do. I just want to make people feel better about themselves."

"That's valuable to society," she said, rubbing my shoulders with both hands.

"Yeah. But it's not…" I waved grandly at the screen. "It's not *lasting societal impact* valuable." I peered up at her. "You think I'm overthinking this, don't you?"

"I didn't say a word." She dropped a kiss on my forehead. "All I'm saying right now is that you'd better get in the shower if you expect to be at your mother's place by 7:30."

I glanced at the screen again. "Is that the time?" I downed the coffee as quickly as I could. Then I stood and took her in my arms. "Have a great day, Hotaru."

"You don't want me to leave, do you?" she said, as I rained kisses across her cheek and started down her neck.

"How did you ever guess?"

She took my face in her hands and got some space between us. Then she trailed her fingers down my torso as low as they could go. "Hold that thought," she said with a sly grin before turning away.

"That was mean!" I called after her. "Giving me a boner before I have to pick up my mother!"

"You need a shower anyway," she called back, and shut the door.

I ran my hands through my curls – man, I needed a haircut – and sniffed at my armpits. Then I looked at the time again. "Crap," I muttered, and bolted for the bathroom.

# Chapter 5

I wondered whether I'd have to wait for Mom to finish getting ready. But she was waiting by the front door for me, practically tapping her foot. "I was just about to call you," she said.

"I'm not late," I said, dropping a kiss on her cheek. "Can I go in to say hi to Dad? I'd like to ask him about something." She gave me the stinkeye, but I rushed to reassure her that it would only take a minute. "It's a guy thing," I said, putting every ounce of sincerity I could into my gaze.

"You know I've seen through that innocent act of yours since you were four," she said. But she stepped aside and let me through. "He's in the kitchen."

More precisely, Dad was at the table, reading glasses perched low on his nose as he read the news on his tablet. "They have more portable devices now, y'know," I said.

"Just what I need," he said. "An even smaller screen, when I can barely see this one."

I slid into a chair. "Level with me," I said, dropping my voice. "What's with Mom?"

His welcoming smile turned sad. "You'll have to talk to her about it. I've been sworn to secrecy."

"Come on," I hissed. "I'm your son! You can tell me!"

"I can't. I'm sorry, Webb. It's up to her."

I focused my gaze on my folded hands atop the table, and tapped my thumbs against one another for a moment. "Just tell me this. Is it bad?" Only then did I look up at my father's face.

Tears glistened in the corners of his eyes. "It's not good," he admitted.

"What's not good?" Mom said from the doorway. I jumped at the sound of her voice.

"Your cooking," said my father, "but that's been true for thirty-five years. Dunno why he's bringing it up now." His tone was light, but he shot me a significant look.

Mom harrumphed and turned away from us. "Let's go, Webb. We'll take my car. It's easier for me to get in and out of."

I glanced between Mom's retreating back and Dad's expression as he watched her leave. He noticed me watching him and shooed me away. "Go on. We'll talk later."

I laced my reply with sarcasm. "You won't tell me anything then, either. I *know* how this *works*, Dad." But I followed Mom anyway.

Mom hadn't been a lawyer for so many years for nothing. She knew full well that I wanted to ask her about her health – and she also knew that the best defense was a stellar offense. "How's your sister?" she shot at me as soon as we both got in the car.

I sighed as I backed up her car. "I have no idea. You know as much about her life as I do."

"She doesn't ever call you? Text you? Post crazy photos to your Facebook page or whatever it's called now?"

"Not for a long time. Not since your last conversation with her." I glanced over at her as I negotiated the turn out of our neighborhood. "What did you two talk about, anyway? I've never heard the full story."

"There's no story. We had a disagreement."

"About what?" I glanced at her again. "Whatever it was, it made her so mad that she stopped talking to all of us. She won't answer my calls or emails. She won't even talk to Hilary." Frustration was getting the better of me, and I knew it, but I found myself unable to keep quiet. "I know you want to keep this stuff private, but that's just not fair, Mom. It's affecting all of us. At least tell me what it's about."

She reared back and glared at me. My implication was clear: *You can talk to me about this thing you don't want to talk about, or we'll discuss the other thing you don't want to talk about. Your choice.*

I'd absorbed more at my parents' dinner table than Mom's cooking, and she knew it.

"Fine," she said. "We talked about the prophecy."

"You'll have to be more specific," I said. In my family, prophecies were as common as dirt. If you weren't under a *geas* of some sort, people wondered whether you were adopted.

"The one about Sage saving the Earth."

That brought me up short. "She did that already. Remember? The gods hollowed out the mountain under Grandfather's old wickiup so They could reverse climate change."

Mom shook her head. "That's what she said, too."

"So wait," I said. "There's more? Facing down a giant iceworm and nearly losing Rafe multiple times weren't enough?"

"It's not my prophecy, Webb," said Mom defensively. "I'm not the one who came up with it."

"Who did?" I asked.

Mom sighed. "The goddess came to me about a year ago and said we weren't done." *The goddess*, in our family, was shorthand for White Buffalo Calf Pipe Woman.

"Oh?"

I saw her nod out of the corner of my eye. "I told Her we were. I said we'd served Her purposes for thirty-five years and counting. Her hand-picked team had gotten the gods to agree to the power-sharing deal that led to the Second Coming, and your father and I had produced the heir She wanted. That heir then went on to stabilize the planet's environment – which was something the gods Themselves hadn't been able to figure out how to do."

"Right," I said.

"And She said Sage wasn't the heir."

"What?" I nearly ran the car off the road.

"She said Sage was Earth's savior, and save the Earth she had. But your father and I were never the ones who were supposed to produce the heir."

"Hang on a minute," I said slowly. "The heir is different from the savior?"

"Apparently."

"So what's the heir's job?"

"The heir," Mom said, "is supposed to administer things on Earth after the gods leave."

I took a moment to digest that bit of news. "So the gods had planned to leave all along," I said. "That's interesting. I wonder why They never explained that part to us."

"Oh, you know how They are," she said, throwing a hand in the air. "They would have shared the news with us eventually, if They thought we needed to know."

Mom always did have a way with sarcasm. "Did you know about this inheritance plan before the goddess spoke to you that time?"

"Nope." Mom turned and looked out the window.

"And who's supposed to produce this heir, if not you and Dad?" I asked, although I was pretty sure I already knew the answer.

Mom didn't turn from the window. "The savior."

"So of course you told Sage."

"What else was I supposed to do, Webb? She needed to know, didn't she?"

I conceded the point, but still. My sister had never wanted any part of this stuff in the first place. She would have given back the laser-eye trick in a heartbeat, and if no one had ever expected her to fly, that would have been fine and dandy. But she'd played along because it was the only way to fix the Earth's climate in time. Now to be told that she was supposed to make a baby on command? "Well," I said as the gate to the Holts' residence opened before us, "that would definitely account for her being mad at all of us."

"I swear to all the gods, Webb," Mom said fiercely, "if I had known when the goddess first showed up in that sweat lodge that all of this was going to be the result, I would have told Her to take a hike."

I had more questions, but no time to ask them; as soon as we hit the front door, Mom was whisked away by some assistant to prepare for the show. I found myself alone and unescorted in the Holts' home, for the first time since I was a kid.

I knew the Holt sons, although we weren't buddies. Both boys had their father's Nordic good looks. Rex, the older one, was six years younger than me, and was in the process of picking up the mantle of the family's political dynasty. He had already won a seat on Denver's city council, and rumor had it that he planned to run for mayor in the next election.

The younger kid, Roman, couldn't have been more different. Mom had once snarked that Roman was the President's true heir; at twenty-three, he had yet to graduate from the University of Denver because he couldn't settle on a major. His favorite things in life appeared to be skiing and women – not necessarily in that order. Sometimes he would wander over to the Sixteenth Street Mall to smoke a joint and play boogie-woogie on one of the out-of-tune street pianos the city provided for tourists. He'd even put out a hat, like a busker, and cackle like mad when some unsuspecting tourist threw him money. He never kept it – he donated it to an on-campus charity. He just liked putting one over on people. And playing boogie-woogie piano.

As if on cue, a rumble of ragtime music issued from the next room over. I ambled in, and there was Roman, seated at a baby grand piano and cranking away. A smile like sunshine creased his face when he saw me. "Hey! Webb, isn't it? How you doin', man?" He half-rose from the piano bench as I approached, and reached out a thin, long-fingered hand for me to shake.

"I'm good, Roman. I'm good. Hey, I'm sorry about your dad."

He waved away my concern as he resumed his seat, smoothing his swoop of bangs out of the way with one hand – a habitual gesture of his that I'd forgotten about. "It's cool. He's back, you know. The whole thing was a big misunderstanding."

My eyes widened in surprise. "Yeah?"

"Yeah. So. You here for the big reveal?" He cocked a thumb toward the other side of the house. Then, seeing my frown of confusion, he grinned even wider. "You mean you didn't know? Sweet! Come on, I'll take you." He stood up and closed the piano.

Then, pushing back his bangs again, he beckoned for me to follow him.

I couldn't help but take in his ripped jeans and fraying Aran sweater as I followed him through the maze of rooms. I assumed he cultivated the look. It's not like his parents couldn't afford to buy him better clothes.

It wasn't long before we passed through an unassuming door into a gallery lined with windows. This spot felt different than the rest of the house; I presumed it had been built around the time the President took office, as a covered walkway between the house and the offices of the President's support staff. A few seconds later, I discovered I'd been right; another unassuming door at the end of this corridor opened onto a typical cube farm, with traditional offices lining the walls around a big open area filled with partitioned workspaces. Most of the offices were dark – an ex-President doesn't need a ton of staff, after all – but the back left-hand corner was all lit up. Roman headed that way.

As we approached, I heard a babble of voices, and then began to pick out individuals I recognized: Mom's first, of course, and then Antonia's, and finally Tess's. We went through a glass door and rounded the end of a matte-black partition, and there, at last, was a brightly-lit stage with Mom, Tess, and Antonia seated in chairs around a plain coffee table. A large plant that may or may not have been fake filled the space between Tess and Mom. Tess hadn't changed a bit since the last time I'd seen her in person, some fifteen years before. Now she was in her early 50s, but even though her short hair had gone gray, she exuded more energy than anyone else I knew – including my mother, which was saying something.

A makeup artist and a lighting guy were fussing around the three women and talking to themselves – or so I thought, until I saw their earpieces. I glanced to my right and discovered a glassed-in booth where a few people were already sitting.

"Roman!" Antonia called, and got up to give her son a hug. That annoyed the lighting guy, but he stood with exaggerated patience, eyes cast to the ceiling as if looking to the gods for strength. *Fat lot of good that'll do you right now.*

I took the opportunity to scoot over to my mother and whisper in her ear, "Roman told me his father's back." I pulled back far enough to see her surprised expression, then leaned in again to say, "He says it was all a misunderstanding."

"What the hell?" Mom murmured to me.

"That's all I know." I straightened and gave her a grin. "Break a leg, Mom."

"I hope you don't expect me to take that seriously," she said. "Antonia! Talk to your boy later. Let's get this show on the road."

"I was just about to say that myself," Tess said, touching her earpiece. "Quiet, everyone. We're live in thirty seconds. Why don't you guys go sit in the booth?"

Roman and I smiled and nodded, and made as if to head that way. But he veered off into the shadows. "I used to do this when I was a kid," he whispered as I followed him. "We'll be fine here, as long as we stay quiet." He smoothed back his bangs and hunkered down in a crouch.

*When in Rome, do what Roman does?* Hilary would have smacked me for the pun, but luckily for me, she wasn't with me. I settled in next to him and awaited developments.

The red light came on atop the robot camera and Tess began the program. "Hello, everyone. This is *Talk About a New Earth* on NWNN, and I'm your host, Tess Showalter. I'm coming to you live from Denver, Colorado, and the home of former U.S. President Brock Holt. With me are his wife, former First Lady Antonia Greco, and a woman who needs no introduction, Naomi Witherspoon Curtis. They have brought dire news to our worldwide audience. Naomi, would you like to start?"

Mom bore no sign of the weakness she'd shown in the car on the way home the day before. She sat up straight and said clearly, "Thank you, Tess, and yes, we have dire tidings indeed. For the past several days, none of us who have alliances with the gods have been able to contact Them – nor have any of Them contacted us."

"They're gone?" Tess asked.

"Apparently."

"Any idea where?"

"What we have is mostly speculation. But early yesterday morning, my son Webb received an indirect message that there may be a battle brewing in the gods' realm. We have no way of knowing what it's about, though, and of course we can't ask the gods for an explanation because…"

"They're not talking to us," Tess put in. "Yes, I see. And I should let our viewers know that no one at NWNN has been able to contact any of the gods for comment." Which meant, I surmised, that neither Darrell nor Tess had heard from their deities, either. That made me sad; Morrigan was a cranky piece of work, but I'd always liked Nanabush.

Tess turned to her other guest. "Antonia, do you have anything to add? Have you heard from your own contact among the gods and goddesses?"

"I have not," Antonia confirmed. "And moreover, sometime last night, Brock vanished."

Tess waited a beat for that to sink in. "You're saying former President Holt has disappeared?"

"That's exactly what I'm saying. He disappeared from his bed…"

"Now, now, Antonia, it's all right." The velvet curtains behind me rustled, and the former President himself strode past me toward the set.

"Dad?" Roman blurted. Then, in a fierce whisper, he said, "That's impossible. Where the hell did he come from?"

"Is there a door back there?" I hissed back.

"No! It's a concrete-block wall!" When I stared at him, he said, "Look for yourself."

So I did. He was right. There was no door behind the curtains near me. I scooted along the wall to see whether some sort of passageway was hidden farther along – and came up short against something tall, warm, and unyielding.

"Steady there, little spider," murmured the voice from my dream.

"Loki!" I hissed.

"So you know me at last," came the teasing response. "I'm *so* relieved. I was afraid we would have to play Twenty Questions, and that would have wasted time you don't have."

"What's going on?" I said, trying to keep my voice down, but not succeeding very well.

"Attend," He said. "All shall be revealed." With that, He strode out from behind the curtains and joined President Holt on the set. I followed Him out, but stopped just outside the brightly-lit portion of the studio.

Then I pulled the loose end of a ball of heavy-duty twine out of a pocket of my cargo pants, and began manipulating it as fast as I could. Loki wasn't the only Trickster here. I just hoped I could outmaneuver him if Mom needed rescuing.

While I was matching wits with Loki behind the curtain, not much had happened on the air. The President and Antonia had had a tearful reunion, and he had assured viewers that he had not been kidnapped. Far from it, in fact. "I went to the gods' realm at Loki's request," the President said, nodding to the Norse Trickster, who joined everyone else on the set and did His best to look like a simple messenger.

"And why did Loki need you there?" asked Tess, doing *her* best to look as if the interview hadn't gone completely off the rails.

"He needed an ambassador. Of course, I have a great deal of experience in the role, as you know, having served for seven years as the U.S. ambassador to France."

*Which he mainly spent on the slopes.* I knew exactly what Mom was thinking.

"Right," Tess said. "And when you were acting as an ambassador in the gods' realm, whose interests were you representing?"

The President actually squirmed. "Actually, it was more of a liaison role."

Mom turned to him. "And who's liaising with whom? Come on, Brock. What's going on up there?"

Loki gave up His just-the-messenger routine and practically shoved the President out of the way. "I called on President Holt," He said, "to help patch the holes in the agreement that *you*, Naomi, negotiated back in 2013."

"Holes?" Mom said, affronted.

"Yes, holes," Loki returned. "Oh, that deal has served Earth pretty well for the past thirty-five years. But nobody can deny that it's showing its age. Humans are beginning to fall through the safety net."

I winced, thinking about the panhandler we'd seen the day before.

"But why Brock?" Mom said, sounding a little desperate. "Why not approach *me*? Why didn't White Buffalo Calf Pipe Woman contact me?"

Loki smirked. "She gave me to understand that the last time She asked you for help, you turned Her down."

Mom regarded Him with narrowed eyes. "That's not true."

He waved his hands. "Anyway, it doesn't matter," He said. "The fact is that many of Us think White Buffalo Calf Pipe Woman has handled the whole thing badly from the start. We have always questioned Her reliance on you and Joseph. And now…"

"And now You have come to make trouble, as usual," said Morrigan, striding out of the shadows to my right. Two steps brought Her next to Tess, with Her sword drawn and pointed at Loki.

"Nothing ever changes, does it, Morrigan?" said Diana, as She took up a place next to Antonia with an arrow already nocked in Her bow.

I shoved the twine back in my pocket. No need for it now, with Them double-teaming Loki.

The Norse god rolled His eyes dramatically. "And I suppose the two of You have been deputized by Odin to tie Me to that rock again."

"Not yet," Morrigan said, Her posture unchanged. "But I'm certain it's only a matter of time. Now take Your lies and begone."

Loki cringed away from Her in mock fear. "All right, yes, I'll go. Mr. President, are you coming with Me?"

"No!" chorused Antonia and Diana.

President Holt shrugged. "I've done as much as I could do, anyway. I think You're in over Your head, Loki. I told You that before."

The god practically snarled at him. "Fine. I shall handle it from here Myself." Then the corners of His lips curved up in a secretive smile. "In any case, My work here is done." And He was gone.

Morrigan straightened and sheathed Her sword. Then She turned to Tess. "Alas, We cannot stay. He is right about one thing: there is a great deal of disagreement in Our realm right now, and He is responsible for only part of it."

"Has Ragnarok come?" Mom asked.

Morrigan's gaze flicked to Diana, who gave an almost imperceptible nod. "If you like," the Irish war goddess said.

I could see Mom getting ready to challenge Her for a better answer, but Diana stepped in. "To be clear, We are not being held hostage, nor have the doors to the gods' realm been locked against humans. But things are very delicate right now, and We are minimizing Our contact with humanity as a precaution. Really, it's for your own safety." Her tone of voice was so sincere that I might have believed Her – had I not flashed on the memory of Iktomi crouched on my deck, looking furtively over His shoulder right before He fled.

"Don't worry about Us," Diana went on with a bright smile. "We'll contact you when it's safe again to do so." She nodded to Morrigan, and both of Them faded out.

The set looked much emptier, devoid of the gods. Mom practically looked puny.

"All right, then," Tess said, "we began our program with more questions than we had answers, and we're ending it with even more questions. *TAaNE* will keep you up to date with all the latest on the war in heaven. Reporting live from Denver, I'm Tess Showalter, and now back to Zane Abdelsamad in Washington."

Three beats later, the red light on the robocam went out, and Tess's shoulders slumped, her gaze fixed on the spot where Morrigan had last stood. Then she shook her head, and turned on Mom and Antonia. "What the fuck was that all about? You didn't bring me out here on false pretenses, did you, Antonia?"

"Of course not," Antonia snapped. "Brock really did go missing. I had no idea he was back."

"I did," Roman said, sidling up to his parents. "Hi, Dad."

"And you didn't tell me?" Antonia demanded.

Roman shrugged. "I didn't know until after you'd all gone into the studio."

"Jesus Christ on a crutch," Tess said, and stood. She looked up at the booth and called, "Let's get going. If we hustle, we can catch the three o'clock shuttle and be home by dinnertime."

"Sounds good to me," someone in the booth said over the intercom.

The Holts were still having a family discussion, complete with raised voices. Tess turned to Mom, who was the only person still seated. "Sorry it all blew up on you," Mom said.

Tess shrugged. "That's show business. Are you gonna be okay?"

"I'll be fine. Webb's my designated driver." She held out a hand so I could help her out of her chair.

# Chapter 6

Mom and I ran into the other missing Holt on our way out. Rex, the favored son – he of the chiseled features and the perfectly-coiffed blond hair – strode toward us with a pack of media types at his heels. They kind of jammed up the gallery between the house and office annex, so Mom and I stopped to see whether they would part in the middle for us.

They didn't. Instead, Rex held up a hand and the whole train came to a halt. "Hello, Naomi. Hello, Webb," the council member intoned in a deep, sonorous voice.

Keep in mind that Sage and I more or less grew up with the Holt kids. Our families weren't besties, but Mom and Antonia liked each other, and the two of them would occasionally come up with a reason why everybody had to get together for a cookout or something. Dad and the President would exchange frosty greetings and take turns glaring at each other for the next couple of hours, and the Holt boys and I would try to antagonize Sage into shooting sparks from her eyes.

Anyway, my point is that I knew what Rex Holt's real voice sounded like, and let's just say he was not a natural baritone. I'd heard rumors that he'd hired a voice coach, but I thought it more likely that Narcissus had taken him under His aegis, given the family history and all.

"How are you, Rex?" Mom said.

He ignored the pleasantry. "Have you seen my mother?" he asked, brows knitted in concern. "I need to be with her. After all, families should be together in trying times."

"Which trying times are those?" I inquired.

His frown deepened. "I heard my father was missing."

"Oh, right. That." I chuckled. "He's back."

Some of the puffery went out of Rex's sails. "Back?"

"Yeah. Just a few minutes ago. On global-ether TV." I nodded toward my mother. "Tess Showalter was interviewing our moms when your dad showed up. We left them together in the studio just now." Then, as if offhandedly, I added, "With Roman."

"*Roman* knew about this?" cried Rex, shocked into using his normal voice.

"Well, that may be overstating it," I began, but Rex was already pushing past us.

"Lovely to see you again," he said, his cultivated baritone back in place. "We'll have to catch up soon. I'll have my scheduler call you." And just like that, the juggernaut was gone.

Mom and I stared at each other for a moment. "Wow," I said finally. "I thought our family was fucked up."

"Language, Webb," she said in a resigned voice, as we resumed our escape.

"Is it just me," I said, when we had put a couple of blocks between us and the Holts, "or does Roman seem like the smartest one of that whole bunch?"

Mom reclined her seat a few clicks and closed her eyes. "No," she said with a sigh, "Antonia's the smartest. But Roman is quicker than he lets on. And I'd bet he knows exactly why his father left. Why else would he have been there today?"

It did seem odd that Roman, of all people, had shown up when he did. "He was there to make sure I followed you to the studio," I said, thinking aloud.

"He was there for more than that," Mom said. "What did he say to you when Brock appeared? All I heard was voices, but I couldn't make out what you were saying."

I thought back. "He called after his father. And then he told me to look behind the curtain, to see for myself that there was no door that Brock could have come through. So I did. And that's when I ran into Loki."

"He wanted all the players in place," Mom said, as if to herself.

"Roman did?"

"No. Loki."

I glanced at her. "Just before He left, He said He had accomplished exactly what He'd set out to do today."

"Yeah. He put us all on notice. And He tried to piss me off."

"Language, Mom," I teased.

She squinted at me and blew me a raspberry. Then she closed her eyes again. "When He said there were holes in the mediated settlement, that was a blatant attempt to make me angry. But He's right. There *are* holes in the Second Coming agreement. Settlements *always* have holes. That's what happens when two sides in a dispute reach a compromise. When conditions become intolerable for one side or the other, then they call in their lawyers and tweak the deal, or come up with a new one." She grinned. "That's how lawyers keep the lights on."

"So you always knew you'd have to mediate a new deal?"

"Well," she said, and paused. "I'd hoped this one would last longer than thirty-five years," she went on ruefully. "And I thought..." Her voice trailed off.

I gave her a few moments to continue the sentence. When she didn't, I said, "You thought what?"

"I thought I'd have help with the next one," she said. She sounded forlorn.

"Like what kind of help?"

"Like someone to take the lead in the negotiations. Someone who's not old and..." She fell silent again.

"Just spit it out, Mom," I said, letting frustration creep into my voice. "What's going on with you? Why is it such a secret?"

She shook her head. "I need to talk to your sister. I need to make things right with her." She raised the seat back with some effort, and turned to me. "Would you contact her for me? She won't talk to me, but I bet she'll talk to you."

"I bet she won't," I said, "but I'll try. And I'll ask Hilary to try, too."

"That's a good idea," said Mom, as if she hadn't rejected it scant hours before. She closed her eyes again, and I thought she'd dozed off. But as we made the turn into our driveway, she snorted. "Brock's family really *is* fucked up, isn't it?"

I chuckled. "It really is."

"Couldn't happen to a nicer guy," she said as she slid out of the car.

Now *that* sounded like Mom.

I was right. Sage still wasn't talking to me. Or at least, she didn't respond to the email I sent her. Or the text. Or the voicemail I left for her. "Mom's got some big news that she wants to share with you first," I said. "It doesn't look good. She even said she's sorry for arguing with you that last time. Please give me a call."

I knew I was stretching things a little; Mom hadn't said in so many words that she was sorry for riling up Sage. But I thought the novelty of the thing alone might get her attention. Regardless, it didn't work.

Hilary stalked my sister's social media hangouts to figure out where a message would catch her eye the fastest – but Sage hadn't updated any of them in months. "It's like she fought with your mother and went to ground," she told me. "Not that I blame her."

"I don't blame her, either," I said. "But come on. At some point, she's going to have to relent."

"You know," Hilary said, "she might not be hiding out from the family. This might have to do with her job."

"Or it started out with her being mad at Mom, and then her job got in the way," I said, warming to the idea. Sage couldn't carry a grudge forever, could she?

Hilary turned back to her laptop. "Rafe hasn't posted anything in a while, either."

I leaned over her shoulder. "Define 'a while.'"

"Maybe a month."

"So the last month could be attributable to their work schedule. That makes me feel better, I think." Hilary was still typing and clicking away. "What are you doing?"

"There are various ways to track someone online who doesn't want to be tracked," she said, as data scrolled up the screen in front of her. "JAF-H/D has some pretty sweet back-end encryption, but even the best systems have a back door."

"Which you looked for, of course."

"Of course," she said. "They offered me a job, remember? I wanted to know what kinds of yahoos I'd be working for."

"My sweetheart, the master hacker," I said fondly, ruffling the hair that covered the nape of her neck.

"Stop it. That tickles." She swatted my hand away. "Aha!" Three clicks and we were in. Somewhere.

"Honey, where are we?" I asked.

"Back end of the JAF-H/D server."

"And we're looking for…?"

"The last activity by either Sage or Rafe. Honestly, Webb. Use your brain."

"You know my brain can't math," I said.

"There's no math involved." She glanced up at me.

"Yeah, there is," I argued, pointing at the screen. "Look at all those numbers."

She rolled her eyes and went back to poking around where she shouldn't be poking.

A thought occurred to me, and I voiced it. "I don't suppose the CIA will be knocking on our door any time soon over this, will they?"

"Nah," she said. "It's the NSA that handles cyberterrorism. Now hush and let me concentrate."

I braced my hands on the back of her chair so I could lean in and rest my cheek against hers. She did a masterful job of ignoring me. "There," she said at last.

"Where?"

She turned toward me, and I took the opportunity to plant a kiss on her lips. "You're incorrigible," she said with a grin. "And that's Sage, right there."

The string of numbers she pointed to didn't look anything like my sister. "How do you know? Never mind; don't answer that. When was she last online at work?"

"Two weeks ago. And the same for Rafe."

I straightened with a sigh. "So they really are unreachable. Maybe Mom will calm down if we tell her that much."

Hilary nodded as she deleted everything that marked her virtual trail. Then she shut down the computer, stood, and stretched. It was fun to watch.

I took her by the shoulders and turned her to face me. "Will our baby be able to math?" I asked plaintively.

She slid into my arms. "Our baby will be amazing," she promised.

I had big plans to sleep in the next morning. Between my early wake-up call of a few days before, and sleeping at my desk the next night, I was ready to make up for it with several hours of uninterrupted shut-eye after Hilary left for work.

But as she was on her way out the door, she asked me about the grant application. "When is the deadline again?" she asked.

I groaned and sat up. "Wednesday. I guess I'd better get up and get to it."

"You can do it, Webb," she said, dropping a kiss on my cheek. "You'll have the most amazing proposal of anyone's."

"Thanks for the moral support," I called after her as she swirled out of the room. As soon as I heard the front door shut, I muttered, "I hope you're right."

Less than half an hour later, I was back at my computer, coffee in hand, staring bleakly at the application form open on the screen. I still had no clue what *lasting societal impact* my installation would have.

The problem was the concept of the project itself. I don't know if you've noticed, but I'm not much of a make-a-serious-statement kind of guy. In keeping with that, my art tends toward the whimsical end of the spectrum. And having grown up with my sister Sage, the environmental engineer, I had an ingrained appreciation for all things ecological. And so – unlike, perhaps, the artist whose work with *lasting societal impact* would actually win this grant – I designed installations that tended to be ephemeral, or at least impermanent. Something that looked fun or quirky at first, but would then degrade naturally in place, until it was one with the Earth again.

This particular project was pretty far out on the silly end of the spectrum. I intended to site it on a peak, or a naturally-defensible cliff. I didn't have a specific site in mind yet, but it's not like Colorado had a shortage of them; I figured once I got the grant, the perfect site would become obvious, and then I could begin rounding up the permissions. The materials would be biodegradable plastics, fabrics and yarns, colored with natural dyes.

But what's it supposed to be, you ask? What would it look like?

Well, it would look like a castle. Towers, pennants, flying buttresses – the works. If all went as planned, it would look like you could move in and be master of all you surveyed. And I hoped people would come to see it – not to move in, of course, but to stand inside and admire the view, and to let their kids play. I could even envision marketing opportunities – kids' costume parties and so forth. Maybe the Society for Creative Anachronism would stage a sword fight in the bailey. They could sell tickets and make it a fundraiser.

And in a few years' time, the whole thing would be gone, as if it had never been there.

My working title was, "The More Things Change…"

But the more I stared at the computer screen, the more the whole project seemed like a metaphor for the Second Coming. The gods came back, and everything changed. They built Their shining castle on the mountainside by cleaning up the Earth and the humans who live here. And now, maybe, it was all falling apart.

Suddenly, I hated my project. I didn't *want* things to change that much. I didn't *want* the Earth to fall apart again. Because if it did, then what was the point of everything my family had been through over the past thirty-five years?

*What lasting societal impact...*

I was on the verge of kicking my stupid project into the next county when my phone made its *you've got email* yodel. And then it did it again. And again.

None of the messages were from either Sage or Rafe; that would have been too simple. But I had two messages from my father, one from Hilary, and one from Roman Holt, of all people. I had no idea how he'd gotten hold of my email address; maybe he'd hacked into his mother's contacts. Anyway, I opened his first, just for the sheer novelty of it.

> *Hey, wow – have you seen this? Did you know about it before?*
> *Roman*

He followed this cryptic message with a link to a video hosting site. I wasn't inclined to mistrust Roman, but I knew better than to click on that kind of link. While I debated what to do next, I opened Hilary's email. Hers was similarly terse:

> *Call me when you've seen this.*
> *All my love, Hotaru*

She included the same link as Roman had. At that point, I figured it was safe enough. But I still had to look at the messages from Dad. He, too, sent the link, together with this:

> *Don't believe everything you see on the internet. Let's talk after you've watched this.*
> *Love, Dad*

Message two said:

*Your mother wants to know if you've heard from Sage. Please call ASAP.*

*Love, Dad*

Calling Mom was already on my list of things to do, right after drafting my grant proposal and stomping my worthless project into smithereens. But now I wanted to know what video had everybody in a tizzy. I clicked on the link and sat back with my coffee.

The first scenes were a montage of shots of my mother in her prime – on stage when Jesus returned; at later events where she spoke for, and with, the gods; representing Tess before Congress. The narrator said:

*Naomi Witherspoon Curtis – cool, calm, collected. Responsible and respected. Or is she?*

The montage fragmented, and then grainy video footage appeared. First was video of my mother, much younger, her blouse unbuttoned as she mewled for attention from an unseen man – but I could tell from his voice that he was definitely not my father. Then another shot, this time of some sort of rumble in a darkened alley. My mother was dressed like a hooker, and a dark-haired man had her slammed up against a brick wall while she appeared to be helping him unzip his pants.

The narrator picked up again:

*Naomi Witherspoon Curtis – hand-picked by the gods to be Their mouthpiece on Earth. Now that you know the truth about her, do you want this to continue?*

*The gods have* **never** *had the best interests of humanity at heart. We intend to put a stop to Them. Join us.*

The video ended with something about a national Neo-Atheist movement, including a website address. A rooster crowed at the very end, just before everything faded out.

I put down my coffee, amazed that I'd managed not to spill any, and called Hilary first.

"You okay?" she asked.

"Yeah. Although I could have lived without that experience."

She paused. "I'm sorry."

"Thanks," I said, rallying. "I'll be fine. It's not like I didn't know my parents knew about sex, or anything."

"Yeah, but still." She paused again. "Have you talked to them?"

"Not yet. That's next. Dad sent me a couple of emails." Reflexively, I looked at the computer screen again. "And so did Roman, weirdly enough. I didn't realize he had my address."

"Who's Roman?"

"Holt. The ex-President's son. We ran into both him and Rex yesterday."

There was mirth in her voice. "Sometimes I forget you're a bigwig who knows all these famous people."

"Sometimes I forget, too," I said.

That made her laugh aloud. Then she said, "How's the project coming?"

"To be honest," I said, "it's starting to sound like a metaphor for the Second Coming. I'm not sure..."

"Andrew Joseph Curtis, don't you *dare* say you're not going to apply for the grant!"

That stung. "I'm going to apply. It's just that maybe I need a different project."

"There's no time!" she said, raising her voice – something she rarely did.

"Wow, okay. You're right." She was, but still. "I just don't see..."

"Webb," she said, more calmly, "don't you think people need to be reminded sometimes that things change? That they should cherish the moment they're in, instead of living in the past or looking ahead to some perfect future that might never happen?"

"Well, yeah, but…"

"Do you think there might be some *lasting societal impact* in creating a moment for people to cherish, knowing full well that it will soon be gone?" She sighed. "I mean, I know why this isn't obvious to you. It's because you spend so much time *in* the future. You already know what's coming around the bend. You live in anticipation."

"Except for when the future involves me," I said, knowing I sounded defensive. "Then I'm as blind as everyone else."

She sighed. "I need to get back to work."

"And I need to call Dad. I love you, babe."

"I love you, too. *Don't* destroy your project."

"Okay."

"Promise me."

"I promise!"

"Okay." She sounded mollified, but only just. "See you tonight." And she ended the call.

I put down the phone and debated the merits of going back on the promise I'd just made her. Destroying something sounded pretty appealing right then. But I glanced again at my emails. "Right. Dad," I said with a sigh.

My father must have been sitting on his phone; he picked up before it even rang on my end. "Thank the gods," he said. "Your mother was afraid you'd disown her. Have you gotten hold of Sage?"

*Well, then, let's just cut right to the chase.* "Good morning to you, too," I said.

"Sorry. It's been a little crazy here."

"I'll bet."

"It's not what it looks like."

"Yeah, you mentioned that in your emails." I paused. "So what is it, then, exactly?"

It was his turn to pause. "You've read your mother's memoirs?"

"Not really," I admitted. "I had to read parts of them for various classes, but I've never read the whole thing."

"Okay," said Dad. "In any of the parts you read, was there mention of someone named Jack Rivers?"

"The Investigator? Sure." Everybody knew the story, or at least the outlines of it. What Mom had called her woo-woo team had consisted of Dad, who was her Guardian; Aunt Shannon, who was the Counselor; and Jack Rivers. Rivers was a filmmaker who appeared out of the blue one day and proceeded to make life difficult for everybody, including my parents. It turned out he was allied with Tezcatlipoca, a Mexica jaguar god whose whole reason for being seemed to involve creating chaos and discord wherever He went. In my mind's eye, I watched the video again, and paid a bit more attention to the man I hadn't recognized. "That was him, wasn't it?" I asked as daylight dawned. "In that video. That was Jack Rivers."

"Yes."

"So how did Mom end up in that alley…?"

Now a grin crept into Dad's voice. "Actually, that wasn't your mother. It was me."

A chuckle bubbled up and spilled over. "You clean up real good, Dad."

"Yeah, thanks," said Dad. "It was Loki's idea to prank Jack for what he did to your mother in the first part of that video." Here, my father's voice turned dark, and I winced. "What we can't figure out is where the videos came from. Jack could have worn a camera and body mic the day he attacked Naomi – technology was sufficiently advanced for that – but we're puzzled about the video from the alley. I know exactly who was there that night, and where they all were standing. I was distracted, but your mother had a clear line of sight, and she swears there was nobody in a position to record anything."

"Security cam, maybe?" I suggested.

"Maybe," said Dad. "But the angle's awfully low. And another thing – where have those tapes been hiding all these years, and why are they only coming out now?"

"Well, the answer to the second part is easy," I said. "They're coming out now to discredit Mom, so she's cut out of mediating a new agreement among the gods and goddesses."

"Which points to Loki," said Dad. "But while He's capable of being that vindictive, it isn't really His style."

I tapped my chin with a forefinger. "Whatever happened to Jack Rivers?"

"No clue," Dad said. "We heard he finished his degree at U.N.M. After that, he seemed to drop off the face of the Earth. And we couldn't have been happier about it."

"Hmm. Apparently someone was able to track him down."

"Or was able to invent a couple of key scenes."

I blinked. "You think those videos were 'shopped?"

"Maybe."

That would require either some pretty elaborate staging or a professional-grade video and animation suite. I set that idea aside to mull over later. Instead, I asked, "What do you know about this Neo-Atheist movement?"

"First I've heard of them. You?"

"I've never heard of them before, either." I glanced at the monitor for the time. "Let me commit a little google-fu and see what I can find on them. That might give us material we can work with to begin to answer some of our other questions."

"Sounds like a plan," he said.

I paused again, but briefly. "Hey, Dad? How's Mom doing?"

He blew out a breath. "Not great. She's really worried Sage will see the tape without a frame of reference. And for the record, son, your mother never worked as a hooker. And she was not raped." He seemed a little defensive on the last point. "That video was heavily edited to make a point. The raw tape, if it still exists somewhere, would tell a very different story."

"I believe you," I said, holding up a hand as if to swear to it.

His tone softened. "I know you do. Let me get back to your mother. And let me know what you find out, okay?"

"Of course," I said, skipping my usual *duh, Dad* response in light of the seriousness of the situation. "And I'll let you know the minute Sage checks in, although I think it's highly unlikely that she will." I explained what Hilary had discovered during her hacking expedition the previous evening, and added, "I doubt Sage has even seen the video."

"I hope you're right," said Dad. "And if she does, I hope she has the sense to call one of us with questions, instead of going off half-cocked."

"Sage? Go off half-cocked? Surely we're talking about two completely different women," I said, laying on the sarcasm pretty thick.

Dad laughed without much humor in it. "I love you, Webb."

"I love you, too, Dad," I replied, surprised. "I'll talk to you soon." As I ended the call, I looked again at my email. Roman's message sat there enticingly, almost demanding that I reply to it. But I resisted the urge, and instead opened a search window.

Hilary knows all about hacking into places where she doesn't belong – but I have my own talents when it comes to dealing with the internet. It's just one big information web, after all, and I'm not allied with Iktomi for nothing.

In moments, I had more information about the National Neo-Atheist Movement than I had ever wanted to know. To say that these guys had no use for the gods was an understatement. It looked like all of the various crazies who had popped up at the time of the Second Coming – you know, the ones who were sure Jesus wasn't the real Jesus, the ones who insisted on believing in their twisted reading of the Bible even after Jehovah told them they were wrong, and the ones who profited from stirring up hatred and fear – all of those nutjobs had united under this Neo-Atheist banner. There didn't appear to be a lot of them, but there were enough to make some noise. Their leader was a young firebrand named T. Warden Proffitt. According to the Neo-Atheists' website, Proffitt wanted to return the world to "a purer time, when white men ruled benevolently, and women and minorities knew their place."

You would think, after all these decades, the gods would have rooted out all these guys who thought the color of their skin gave them the right to be in charge. Alas, apparently They had missed a few.

I heard the front door open and shut; in another moment, Hilary entered the studio, and I stood and welcomed her home. "Tough day at the office, babe?" I asked, nuzzling her neck.

"Sort of," she said, stepping back a little. "It was hard to concentrate while everyone was buzzing about that video of your mom, but trying not to be so loud as to interrupt me." She rolled her eyes. Then she frowned at something over my shoulder. "Where did you find *that?*" She indicated my monitor, where I still had the Neo-Atheists' website up.

"That's the group that made the video," I said, trailing across the room after her. "Or the group that claimed responsibility for it, anyway."

"Not that," she said. "Him." She pointed at the photo of T. Warden Proffitt as if he were something she might have found stuck to her shoe.

"He's their leader," I said.

"He's a fucking asshole," she said.

I blinked, hard. Hilary doesn't usually resort to such strong language. "You know him?"

"Yeah, I know him." She turned toward me. "I dated him in high school, until he tried to set fire to Enkou."

"He did *what?*"

"Tried to set fire to Enkou," she repeated. "He did time for it, too. Enkou made sure of that."

"Giving a Japanese god a hotfoot is not your smartest move," I said.

"Nope." She scrolled down the page. "Uh-oh. Hey, Webb?"

"Yes, babe?"

"You know how I said Sage and Rafe had last checked in at work about two weeks ago?"

"I remember. What about it?"

"Well," she said, "they checked in from a site near Greenville, South Carolina." She tapped the bottom of the screen. "And Ward's outfit is headquartered there."

I spent about ten seconds visualizing Sage confronting a guy who believed women should know their place, and shook my head. "This is not going to end well for him, is it?"

"Nope," she said, and laughed. "I wish I could be there to see it."

## Two weeks earlier...

I could see Rafe watching me out of the corner of my eye. I thought he'd come up with some crack about my driving, but he stayed quiet. It was hard to ignore, but I managed it – if only for about fifty miles.

Then I broke. "Stop staring at me. If you have something to say, spit it out."

"I'm not staring at you."

"Bullshit."

"I'm trying to figure out how to phrase what I want to say."

"Don't bother. Darrell's already said it all." I'd been distracting myself from Rafe's stare – or trying to, anyway – by mulling over the briefing we had received from our boss before we got in the car.

Darrell hadn't pulled any punches. "Out of everyone on this team, you two are best suited for this project," he said. He always called our assignments projects instead of missions, so we wouldn't think we were working for the CIA or something. It didn't really work, but it made him feel better. Anyway, he said, "But I have reservations about sending you."

"We'll be fine," Rafe had protested. "Nothing will go wrong."

"*You'll* be fine," Darrell said. "It's Sage I'm not so sure about."

I'd set my lips in a determined smile – as I was doing right now, remembering – as I informed my supervisor in no uncertain terms that he could count on me.

He shook his head. "You're not getting it, Sage."

"Oh? What am I not getting?"

He pointed at me. "That, right there, is what I'm talking about. You cop an attitude at the slightest provocation. You cannot do that on this project."

"I won't!"

"And now you're arguing with me." He shook his head. "You're not setting my mind at ease here."

I closed my eyes before I shot sparks at him. "I realize that I will have to behave differently when Rafe and I are embedded. I know these men expect their women to be subservient."

"And submissive," Rafe put in. "Don't forget submissive."

"Stop acting like you're going to enjoy this," I shot back.

"Hey, I'm going to have the upper hand for once," he said with a grin. "It's likely to be a long time before I have this opportunity again. I intend to enjoy it."

"Yeah, well, if you enjoy it too much, you may find yourself in divorce court as soon as we get back." I turned back to Darrell. "Sir." I knew I was being a smartass, but for some reason I couldn't stop myself. The whole idea of this mission rubbed me the wrong way. We were supposed to infiltrate a colony of white supremacist whackjobs with Neanderthal attitudes about women and find out all we could on their operation – their numbers, their leadership, and their eventual goal. I was on board with all of that. What I couldn't stomach was the idea that I'd have to put my personality on hold for however long it took to get the info. Darrell put the initial time frame at two weeks, but it was a ballpark figure. We might have to stay longer – or if something went wrong, we might have to pull out in a hurry. And now Darrell was implying that I was the most likely reason things would go wrong.

The thing was, he was right. Which was part of why I was so pissed off.

He studied me with an unreadable expression. "Sir?" I said again.

"There was a time in my life," he said gently, "when anger was my go-to reaction to everything. I felt like the gods had yanked me off my life's path and forced me onto a collision course with everything I despised. I had to choose – either make the best of it or be angry at everyone all the time."

"Even Nanabush?" Rafe asked.

"Especially Him. He was the one doing the yanking." A rueful smile flashed across his face.

"Hard to believe anyone could be angry at Nanabush," I allowed. The lop-eared Potawatomi culture hero was one of my favorites among the gods. He seemed so human sometimes.

"But I was. Feel free to ask Him about it. I'm sure He'd be more than happy to tell you what a seriously unpleasant son of a bitch I was."

"So what changed?" I asked. He'd caught me up in his personal story so thoroughly that I forgot to be mad at him, the rat bastard.

"The gods whacked me upside the head a few times," he said, the rueful smile back in place.

"How many times?" Rafe asked, his eyes lit with mischief.

"Too many. Way too many." Darrell turned to me. "What I'm saying, Sage, is that I hope it doesn't take you as long to figure it out as it took me." He nodded toward Rafe. "Time's a-wastin'."

I still couldn't figure out what he'd meant by that. Now, in the car on the way to Greenville, I glanced over at Rafe. "What did Darrell mean, anyway, when he said time was wasting?"

Rafe suddenly looked uncomfortable. "Uh…I'm not sure."

"Make a guess."

He shifted – squirming, almost. "Look, honey, I love you very much. You know that, right?"

My stomach lurched. "Maybe I *don't* want to hear this."

His features twisted. "I'm not…it's not… Look." He put his hand over mine atop the gearshift lever. "It's hard for me, sometimes. You're so quick to criticize. Every time I get excited about something, you're right there to poke holes in it and tell me why it won't work."

I glanced over at him in disbelief. "You want me to be your cheerleader? Look, Rafe, I love you, too – but we're in this marriage together. I think I have a duty to tell you when I think something won't fly. Don't you? I mean, I want you to be successful."

"Because a rising tide lifts all boats."

"Exactly."

"Did your mother raise you this way?"

I looked sharply at him. "How did this get to be about my mother?"

"I'm just trying to figure out where this habit of yours came from. Some people have loved ones who support them unconditionally."

"And let them make stupid mistakes."

"How else do people learn?"

I shook my head. "Not good enough. I hate making mistakes. I'd rather someone talk me out of a massive screw-up before it happens." I hooked a thumb at myself. "Engineer here, remember? Failures mean dire consequences. People might even die." I didn't need to remind him of what had happened when we'd tried to encourage the growth of shelf ice around Greenland.

"Failure isn't the end of the world, Sage," he said quietly. "And there's no reason to snap at me."

"I wasn't..."

He sighed. "Darrell was right. You can't rein in your anger for even a minute. This project is going to go down in flames." He looked out the window.

"No, it won't," I said, only dimly aware that I had just contradicted him again.

The rest of the six-hour drive was strained, but civil.

JAF-H/D had provided us with a beater of a hovercar whose title had been scrubbed. DMV records on the car now indicated it had been bought new, ten years before, by Ted and Gemma Wodehouse – a fine, upstanding couple from Gainesville, Virginia, who had recently fallen on hard times, Ted having been laid off by a tech firm about six months previously. Our pal Grady had been posting online as Ted for the past several months, making a target of himself by complaining about how the gods seemed to be holding men back from their rightful place in the world. Eventually somebody pointed him toward the Neo-Atheists, and "Ted" quickly moved into the online inner circle by offering to do some non-secure computer programming tasks for them. Grady watched them try to poke holes in "Ted's" story via their background check, and was inordinately proud of himself when his secret identity passed the perps' tests with flying colors. That was when Ted was issued an invitation to meet the big brass at the home office.

Our local agents had already checked out the address; it was nothing but a vacant lot. The real operation was somewhere in the sparsely-populated mountains west of Greenville, most likely over the state line in Georgia.

Our mission was to meet our contact at the bogus headquarters and see what happened. We assumed we'd be told to abandon the car, as Ducky's erstwhile parishioners had done, and someone would drive us to the actual site from there.

"Why didn't the gods clean out all these nutjobs when They first returned to Earth?" I'd asked Darrell early on. I'd had a feeling, even then, that this was going to end up inconveniencing me in some way.

He smiled briefly. "You have to understand that there were a lot of moving parts," he said. "The gods can't be everywhere, all the time – as you, of all people, know from personal experience. They recruited human helpers to handle some of the smaller stuff, while They Themselves went after the worst offenders. I think They believed that if They cleaned up the major problems, it would go a long way toward fixing everything else."

"Trickle-down morality, in other words," I'd said.

"That's one way to put it."

"And it worked about as well as the economic variety."

"Better, actually. A lot of stuff did get cleaned up. And JAF-H/D was created to facilitate the process; we're supposed to be where the gods can't."

I wrinkled my nose at the bureaucratese. "Which is why we're still putting out fires, thirty-five years on?" I'd asked. "Wouldn't it have made more sense to root out all these elements at the start? Then we wouldn't have to do it now."

His lip curled. "You make it sound so easy," he said, and turned away.

The answer didn't satisfy me, but he didn't appear to have another that would have made me feel any better.

We reached our destination just past dark. We'd switched drivers some miles out of town, in keeping with the idea that the husband should always be in charge. We'd also changed clothes at that stop; now, under a thrift-store winter coat, I wore a flowered dress with a modest neckline and a hemline that hit below the knee. The dress was probably the least flattering article of clothing I'd ever worn. Rafe, for his part, sported a pair of khaki slacks with a dress shirt and tie, with a similarly run-down topcoat. We had ditched our own clothes at the rest area where we'd stopped to change, and hoped these Neo-Atheists weren't tracking us on our way down.

Rafe slowed as we turned onto the street where the headquarters supposedly was located, as if looking for an address. He stopped altogether at the vacant lot, then crept farther along the street as if to confirm he'd had the right place.

"Did you see them?" he asked me as he pulled around the corner to circle the block and make another pass.

I nodded. "Two vehicles with their lights off, parked in the lot." I glanced behind us. "One of them pulled out behind us."

"I see him," he said, looking in the rear-view mirror. "Want to bet that the other guys will head us off in a minute?"

"Nope."

And a few seconds later, Car Number Two rounded the corner ahead of us and pulled into our lane, the driver flashing his headlights at us. We pulled over obediently, and Rafe put on a confused expression as he rolled down the window. "What's this all about?" he called to the man getting out of the car that faced us.

The man approached our car and rested his forearms on Rafe's open window. "Good evening. Can I see some identification?" He spoke with an Appalachian lilt.

"Are you police?" my husband asked. In reply, the man simply held out his hand for Rafe's – I mean Ted's – ID. Rafe handed it over; the man glanced at it and handed it back.

"Mr. and Mrs. Wodehouse?" he asked.

"Yes," Rafe said, nodding. "I'm Theodore Wodehouse, although everybody calls me Ted. This is my wife, Gemma. Can you help us? I think we're lost. We were looking for an address back there…" He hooked his thumb back the way we'd come, and was about to explain about the missing building when the stranger interrupted us.

"We've been expecting you," he said, his face expressionless. "Please follow me." Without another word, he got back in his car, executed a three-point turn, and led us out of town, with the second car following us.

We drove for about another half-hour before heading into a state park – the same one, I noted, where the Barnsteads had ditched their car. Our leader veered sharply left, onto a dirt road that led to an overlook that I was sure would be much more picturesque – as well as less scary – in daylight. The man got out of his car and directed us to pull into a spot between some trees, which Rafe did. Then he got out of the car, leaving the door open. I stayed put.

The car's overhead light poorly illuminated the scene. But from where I sat, I could see Rafe's back and the shadowy figure who approached him now. The second car cut his headlights and stayed well back from the scene; I assumed he was the lookout.

"Listen here," Rafe said to the man, "I'd like to know what this is all about. You seemed to know we were coming, but you haven't introduced yourself or anything. And now you've brought us out here to the gods know where…"

"First off," the man said, "it would be a good idea for you to drop any references to the gods from here on out."

"Of course," said Rafe. "It was just a figure of speech."

"I understand, but don't do it," the man said. "Mr. Proffitt won't take kindly to it."

Rafe made a show of looking around. "Is he here? When do I get to meet him?"

"We're to take you to him," the man said. "But you need to leave your car here. Don't worry – we'll move it to a safe place for you. Grab your bags, and then you and your missus come on."

Rafe ducked his head back into the car. "Gemma, we need to go with this man. He's going to take us to Mr. Proffitt."

"What about the car?" I asked, as demurely as I could.

"We're to leave it here. Come on. It's going to be fine."

Slowly, I got out of the car. It had gotten chilly now that the sun had set; I could see my breath. I kept my eyes downcast as Rafe collected our battered suitcases from the trunk. Then he took my hand and led me to the man who had done all the talking.

"Well, well, well," the man said. "Your wife is a fine-looking woman, Mr. Wodehouse. Congratulations on your good taste." It was too dark to see his face, but the smirk in his voice came through loud and clear. I flashed him what I hoped was a modest smile.

"She's a keeper, all right," said Rafe, sounding very much like an angler who had caught the biggest fish of the day. It was all I could do to keep from kicking him.

"You may call me Mr. Smith," the man said.

"Pleased to make your acquaintance, Mr. Smith," I said.

"And yours, Mrs. Wodehouse. Now let's get moving. Mr. Proffitt is waiting for us." He ushered us to his car and held the back door open for us. Rafe slid in first. As I'd expected, Mr. Smith gave me a little feel up my backside on the pretense of helping me into the car. I restrained myself from slapping him.

As Mr. Smith shut the door after me, I realized there was no door handle on the inside of my door. I exchanged a swift glance with Rafe. *No way out,* I sent to him in our mind-speech.

*I saw that. I wonder if they've had people who have tried to bolt on them.*

*Maybe. Or maybe they saved the extra-special ride for us.*

We exchanged another glance, and I slipped my hand into Rafe's. I didn't have to fake the fear that had begun to bubble up from my gut. Not for the first time, I wondered whether we were getting in over our heads.

# Chapter 7

That night – as if I hadn't been getting little enough sleep already – I had another nightmare.

Once again, I was in the world of icy castles and hatchet-faced blonds. Just as before, they began to follow me as I picked up my pace to get out of their town. This time, however, neither Loki nor the smoke monster appeared. Perhaps Loki had done His part by planting the seed for my recurring hallucinations. I had no rationalization for the smoke monster's absence, but I was also disinclined to look that particular gift horse in the mouth.

Not that I considered the monster a horse, gift or otherwise.

With the black barrier gone, I was able to see where I was going this time. Before me, at the end of this road of ice, was a massive blue castle, bigger than any structure I'd passed so far, and flying a flag – blue, with a red-and-white cross – from the top of its highest crenellated tower. The place was so huge that I assumed the ruler of this region lived there.

As I neared the castle, the people behind me began to chant, "Ingrid! Ingrid!" They kept it up even after I reached the end of the road: the lip of the moat that surrounded the place, as wide as a river and as deep as a chasm. I halted – I hardly had a choice – and felt the crowd surging at my back. I froze in panic, sure the people behind me would push me over the brink.

Directly across the moat from me, the castle's portcullis began to open, and the longest drawbridge I'd ever seen began to fall across the moat. It landed with a thud, the leading edge mere inches from my toes. At that, the crowd's excitement heightened until they were screaming this woman's name.

At last, their frenzy was rewarded – or so I assumed, because they began to cheer as a slender blonde woman stepped from the open portal onto the bridge. She was tiny, shorter even than Hilary, and had the sort of ethereal beauty that made me think she might be fey. But no – the closer she got, the more apparent it was that she was human. And a modern human, at that. She walked with a confident stride, and wore slacks with a sweater in a beautiful ice-blue colorwork pattern that I recognized as Icelandic. I did a bit of a double-take, and checked the flag flying above her castle again. Sure enough, it appeared to be the flag of Iceland.

I'd never been to Iceland myself, but I had friends in college who had gone there over a winter break to experience the midnight sun. They brought back stories of naked orgies in thermal springs under the aurora borealis, and photos – not of the naked orgies (which, to be honest, still disappointed me), but of Reykjavik lit up like a beacon of civilization in an eternal night. So I knew for sure that nobody in Iceland lived in a glacier, or for that matter in a crenellated castle made of ice.

"Ingrid," I said as she approached me.

"I know you," she said. "You're the spider who haunts my dreams." And as she spoke, her face began to morph, shifting into a creepy parody of a child's playful smile. I shuddered, reconsidering whether she might be fey, after all, and tried again to back away. But the crowd kept shoving me forward as her mouth widened into a maw that might have been big enough to swallow the whole world. As I pushed back with all my strength, a glimmering thread dropped between us.

I knew a lifeline when I saw one. I reached up to grasp it, as the expression on her face turned from triumph to dismay –

And awoke with a death grip on Hilary's arm. "Webb?" she asked, voice muzzy with sleep.

I forced myself to peel my fingers away from her arm. "Just a dream, babe. Go back to sleep."

She mumbled something and rolled over, taking my hand in hers. I wrapped her in an embrace and listened for her breathing to deepen and her grip on my fingers to relax.

I had nearly dropped back to sleep myself when my offspring kicked me so hard that I grunted aloud. "Hotaru?" I asked quietly.

But she slept on. Apparently the wake-up call was only for dear old Dad.

I sighed and gave up. It looked like the only person who would be getting any sleep would be the mother of my child. I slipped out of bed, shrugged on a t-shirt and sweatpants, and left our room as quietly as I could.

Then I stood in the hallway, deciding what to do. The living room couch beckoned; it wasn't as comfortable as the bed I'd just left, but my kid wouldn't be able to kick me awake there, and maybe the dreams wouldn't be able to find me, either. I considered sitting out on the deck for a little while, but I knew it would be cold – the forecast had warned of a chance of snow showers – and to be honest, I didn't think I was ready for another bracing chat with Iktomi of the Shadows.

A glimmer of light appeared in the air before me – a gossamer strand that glowed golden in the dark hallway. It looked so much like the lifeline in my dream that I caught my breath. I looked up to see where it had come from. Was there a shining spider spinning the strand above my head? No, it seemed simply to recede into the darkness.

I reached out to touch it with a forefinger. As if that were the sign it had been waiting for, it swung away from me and landed on the floor. Then it extended down the hall toward the back of the house – not toward the deck, but toward my studio. It stopped there, as if waiting for me to follow.

I sighed and ran both hands over my face, rubbing sand from my eyes. I had a feeling it was going to be a very long night.

Morning found me asleep again at my keyboard. When Hilary touched my shoulder, I exploded from my chair, nearly clocking her with my forearm.

"Whoa," she said, backing away. "How much coffee have you had this morning?"

I dropped back into the chair and rubbed at my eyes with my fingertips. "None. I couldn't sleep after the nightmare, and ended up in here." Why I hesitated to tell her about the glowing lifeline, I didn't know, and didn't feel up to figuring it out.

"What nightmare?"

I looked up at her – her open, caring face, and her bulging abdomen – and found I couldn't bring myself to tell her about the woman in my dream, either. "It wasn't a big deal. Never mind. I'll go start the coffee."

She placed a hand on my arm as I passed. "Honey? What's going on?"

"I don't know," I complained, knowing I sounded like a toddler. "All I know is that I can't seem to get a decent night's sleep anymore."

She had moved past me to the monitor. I must have jostled the mouse when I got up, because the screen had lit up to show the web page I had been looking at when I fell asleep: an aerial map of a swath of New Mexico desert. She looked at the map for a moment, and then looked at me.

It wasn't fair to exclude her, and I knew it. "How soon do you have to leave for work?"

"I don't. It's Saturday."

I'd totally lost track of what day it was. "Okay," I said. "Let me start the coffee and I'll tell you what I know."

It was a short conversation. Unlike Sage and me, Hilary had actually read my mother's books; as soon as I told her that Dad had mentioned Jack Rivers, she knew instantly who he was – and had a better inkling than I did of what it meant. "Do your parents think Rivers is behind the attack ad?" she asked.

"They don't know what to think. But I think it's likely that either he or someone else has accessed his raw video. The thing Dad can't figure out is how the video could exist at all. Mom says no one else was in her office during the attack except her and Rivers, and Dad says he would have known if someone was nearby during the incident in the alley."

"Could one of the gods have done it?" Hilary asked. "Rivers was allied with Tezcatlipoca. He's a Trickster, too. And He seemed like the type to pull that kind of prank."

I shrugged. "Maybe. It doesn't really matter now, though. What matters is that the video exists, and there may be more out there. And Mom and Dad have an interest in finding the source and making it stop."

Hilary said slowly, "And you think the source may be somewhere in the New Mexico desert?"

"Maybe," I said, and described the glowing line that had led me to the computer in the middle of the night. "When I fired up the machine, the browser went automatically to a search page I hadn't created – and the first link was to that map you saw a few minutes ago. There was a glowing dot right in the middle of the screen." I'd been playing with my empty coffee mug as I spoke, watching my hands as I passed it back and forth between them. Now I looked up at Hilary. "I think I'm supposed to go there."

I could tell she was in what she called her info-gathering mode. There was no judgment apparent in her expression as she nodded. But she said, "It sure looks like somebody wants you to go there. But I'm hearing a lot of maybes. Who's telling you to do it? Iktomi?"

"I don't think so," I said. "I don't think I've dealt with this entity before."

She nodded again. "Good or bad?"

I smiled half-heartedly. "I don't sense any nefarious intent, if that's what you're asking."

"But it could be a trap."

"Anything could be a trap."

"True." She looked off over my shoulder for a moment. "What about the grant app?"

"Yeah," I said. I'd been wrestling with that bit of timeline myself. "I don't intend to be gone that long. It's a day's drive down, and another day's drive back. I can't imagine it will take more than a day to figure out what's going on down there. So three days, tops." I looked down at my empty mug again. "If I leave now, I'll be back by dinnertime on Monday, and the app's not due 'til Wednesday. I'll have plenty of time to finish it."

"Take Fossil," she said. "That will cut your travel time in half."

I looked up in surprise. "You think I should go?"

She threw up her hands in a way that reminded me of both my mother and my sister. "Webb, honey, I don't know what to think. But your instincts always seem to lead you in the right direction. And I can't stop you from going anyway – you're a grown man, and I have no claim on you."

*Other than the child I'm carrying.* She didn't have to say the words; I knew she was thinking them, and she knew I agreed with her. We had pledged to raise our child together as soon as we found out she was pregnant, regardless of whether we ever formalized our relationship before the gods and everybody.

She hadn't given me the ringing endorsement I was hoping for, but the conversation had gone better than I had expected it would. "Thanks, babe," I said. "I feel like I have to do this – for my parents, and in some weird way, for the Earth, as well." I grinned at last. "And maybe I'll come up with a kickass response to that damned question while I'm on the road."

"Stranger things have happened," she said with a small smile.

If I had known in advance that I was going to take the Fossil on a ten-hour journey into the desert and back, I would have had somebody look it over first.

I've mentioned that this particular vehicle had been my parents'. Mom had insisted on buying one as soon as they were available to the general public, even though the first model was only available in a two-seater – hardly practical for a family.

Three decades later, hover technology had left our little vehicle in the dust, and my parents had purchased more practical versions in the intervening years. But even now, this little car caused heads to turn when I took it out for a spin – not because of its sleek design or its cutting-edge technology, but because it still got off the ground.

Well, most of the time, it got off the ground. Sometimes it didn't. Hence the name Fossil.

Hilary had her own car – a practical and far more reliable four-door with real wheels. The hovercar was mine, more or less, because I didn't do much except run errands around Boulder, with an occasional trip to Golden or sometimes Denver – nowhere that I couldn't get a lift if the car crapped out on me.

Despite its age, Fossil was pretty zippy, and it was fun to bypass traffic jams by levitating over them, even though the spendy airspace tolls made the experience less fun later. Still, I was looking forward to hitting the road as quickly as possible. I downloaded the route to the GPS on my phone and packed a change of socks and underwear, while Hilary threw together a couple of sack lunches and filled several bottles with water. I saw her wipe her eyes more than once, and knew she was thinking of how many times she had brought along emergency bottles of water for the top of Enkou's head. The kappa still hadn't made an appearance, and I was starting to get pissed off at him. He was a kappa, for gods' sake, not an integral part of the gods' political machinations. I was surprised They had involved him at all.

When I saw her put a knuckle to her eye for the third time, I took the bottle from her hand and slipped her a tissue. "He'll come home," I said. "He always does."

"I know. It's just that he's never been gone so long before." She leaned her head on my chest. "And now you're leaving, too."

"Whoa, hey there," I said. "It's only for the weekend, and I'll have my phone the whole time. If you need me, call, and I'll come right back."

She looked up at me. "Promise?"

I squinted at her. "Yes, of course I promise. What's gotten into you, Hotaru?"

"I wish I knew." She shook her head as if to dispel the fear I'd seen in her eyes, and became businesslike again. "Don't pay any nevermind to me, honey. I'm just being silly. Must be the pregnancy hormones. Here." She handed me the bag full of provisions and grabbed another for the water bottles.

As we loaded everything into the car, I took a good look at her, as if to memorize everything about her: the determined expression on her delicate features, the long hair that she kept shoving out of her eyes with her small, slim fingers. I loved her as much in that instant as I ever had, and I almost asked her to come with me.

But I didn't. Which, as it turned out, was probably a smart move.

"I'll be back by tomorrow night," I said. "I promise."

"I believe you," she whispered.

I'd be lying if I said I wasn't excited about this solo trip that Somebody had dropped into my lap. Don't get me wrong – I love my family and I love my life, most of the time. But sometimes it's good to get away. Travel broadens the mind, as they say. And you can do a lot of thinking while you're alone on the road, putting miles of pavement behind you.

I left I-25 at Walsenburg and headed west on U.S. 160. Fossil flew up into the San Juan National Forest with nary a cough or wheeze; I dodged trucks, airborne sledges, and the occasional cow while I mulled over that damned grant app.

Hilary was right when she said that I live in anticipation; watching events unfold as I knew they would was a source of glee for me, most of the time. But she was wrong when she assumed that meant I didn't appreciate the present moment, or take delight in the times when things didn't go the way I thought they would. I was fully aware of the world's impermanence.

And again, I *never* knew how things would turn out if I had a role to play. Back when my sister was mulling over whether to help Rafe with his climate-change project, I could have told her that in the end, the gods would step in and the Earth would be saved. I offered to tell her, in fact, but she declined. Anyway, my point is that had she taken me up on my offer, I could have told her we'd be okay in the end, but not how we would get there. There was a big blank space between *now* and success, because I was destined to be involved.

This time – even with the dubious help of my nightmares – I didn't even have a clue how it would all end. Which indicated to me that my role was going to be freaking huge.

This realization didn't cheer me up. Not only that, but I also realized I'd skated off the subject of the grant app again. Gritting my teeth, I re-trained my attention to the subject at hand.

Impermanence. Appreciation for things that are here for only a short time. Wasn't that a job for marketers? *Now, for a limited time, you can get this nifty thing you never knew you needed for a low, low price…*

Maybe music would provide a better comparison. I'd heard tales of the old days, when people had to hover over their computer keyboards to click at the precise nanosecond when tickets to a particular concert went on sale. Then there was the anticipation of the event, which might be months away…and then the day came at last…and after a couple of hours, the whole thing was over, and you went home with your ears ringing and a big smile on your face. Maybe someone had recorded the show so you could watch it again later. But most likely, no one had. The evening would live on only in your memory.

There was value in that, surely? The morals to that story were legion: good things come to those who wait; precision counts when trying to defeat a ticket-buying bot; life is meant to be lived, not experienced only through a viewfinder; all good things must end.

Like the gods' return to Earth.

I'd made the left turn onto U.S. 550 at Durango while my brain was on autopilot, and now I realized I'd passed the "Welcome to New Mexico – Land of Enchantment" sign some miles back. Traffic had thinned, and I wondered whether I'd either missed a turn, or taken a turn I should have skipped. I glanced at the GPS on my phone, and nearly nosedived into a prickly pear cactus. Normally, the mapped route would show up as a blue line – but overlaid on the blue now was a thin thread of glowing gold.

I stopped for fuel south of Bloomfield and checked the route ahead. It appeared I had at least another hour of driving ahead of me, on roads that looked more like suggestions – and then, it appeared, my lifeline left the blue line entirely and struck off southwest across the open desert. By then, I figured, it would be dusk.

When I went in to pay for the fuel, I asked the clerk about motels nearby. "Farmington's going to be your best bet," the clerk said, nodding back the way I'd come.

"That's what I figured. Thanks." I headed back to the car, squinted at the angle of the sun, and decided to go for it.

I should explain here that Fossil was a dual-hover vehicle. In most day-to-day driving situations, maglev is what you use to fly. You'd have to ask my sister the engineer exactly how it works – but as I understand it, the car powers up a bunch of electromagnets that push against the strips of metal embedded in the pavement. In the early days of hover technology, though, the government was still in the process of retrofitting all the roads with metal strips. So just like every other hovercar built back then, Fossil had a secondary system of duct fans that created a cushion of air for the car to float on. The air cushion wouldn't get you as high off the ground as maglev would, but it did work. And once upon a time, I knew, Fossil's air-cushion system had worked. I had no idea whether it still did, though. I hadn't used it since driver's ed.

So when the time came to go off-roading, I flipped the switch to cut over for the air-cushion system and held my breath. The skirt dropped into place with a *whirr-thunk* and the fans spun up. When I got the green indicator on the dashboard, I cut the maglev and left the road behind.

I'd forgotten how bumpy off-roading was – and how much fun. I whooped like a cowboy as I made Fossil flatten grama grass, dodge sagebrush, and leap dry washes at a single bound.

It lasted about twenty minutes. Then the fans failed, one by one.

Red lights blazed across the dashboard as an obnoxiously loud klaxon announced that the emergency override had kicked in, lowering the wheels and locking them in place. I swore once. Then I concentrated on steering, making sure I didn't end up nose-down in a wash before I could bring the car to a stop.

In the end, I didn't need to hit a wash. The right wheels rolled up over something big – I never did figure out what it was – and tipped the car enough to flip it sideways. All the airbags fired as Fossil and I rolled a couple of times, fetching up against a stand of juniper with enough momentum for the car to bounce back onto the wheels, whereupon a tire promptly blew.

I shut off the engine and sat, breathing hard, as the airbags deflated. That took a minute or two. Then I checked my phone, and stared at the GPS. Either I had managed an amazing navigational feat or the glowing thread had recalibrated to my current location; in any case, I was still on track for my destination. Wherever that was.

And I still had a long trip ahead of me. And it was growing dark.

I knew better than to try to navigate unfamiliar terrain under these conditions. I found my backpack and pulled out a bottle of water and one of the sandwiches Hilary had made for me that morning. Once those were gone, I leaned my seat back as far as it would go, which wasn't very far – it was a really tiny car – and resigned myself to an uncomfortable night.

The sun, shining full in my face, woke me up. I sat up and groaned. My neck hurt from being cocked at an unnatural angle all night, and my right leg had fallen asleep.

I pushed the door open as far as it would go, and tumbled out into the chill of a high desert morning.

"Well, crap," I said aloud as I surveyed my surroundings. I was tempted to go back the way I'd come. The roadway I'd left on my cross-country jaunt was only twenty miles or so behind me, back, uh, that way. Or maybe that way.

I reached into the car for my phone and stopped, realizing I didn't need GPS. For stretched out in front of me was my thin, gold lifeline.

"Okay, fine," I muttered. "I get it. Hang on a sec." I stuffed the rest of my food, and as many water bottles as would fit, into my backpack. Then I pocketed my phone and began walking southwest, following the golden strand.

Just steps from the car, I noticed my little spider pal had hooked himself onto my backpack strap. He raised a leg to wave at me. Feeling somewhat foolish, I waggled my fingers back at him and kept walking. I didn't know where I was going, but at least I had company for the journey.

# Chapter 8

It felt as if I'd been walking for hours, although it was not yet midday, when my spider pal started getting a little crazy. He ran up my arm and across my shoulders, then climbed into my tangled mess of curls to perch on top of my head. He must have found an anchor up there somewhere, because the next thing I knew, he was dangling by a thread in front of my eyes. I could hear him chittering as his legs waved in all directions at once.

"I thought it was only female spiders who spun webs," I said – the first words I'd spoken since striking out from the car. My throat was dry, my lips parched. But when I stopped to get a bottle of water out of my pack, my little pal went into a frenzied dance.

"All right, all right," I rasped, and put the pack back on. "I'm going. But if I die of dehydration out here, I'm blaming you."

As I topped the next rise, I began to wonder whether I was hallucinating in earnest. For there before me, amidst a lopsided circle of yucca in full bloom, was a Navajo-style loom. The thing was enormous – big enough to make a room-size rug, at least. The rug strung upon it was not far along; only a couple of inches showed at the very bottom of the loom. And seated before it, on a stack of folded rugs, was the weaver: a gray-haired woman in a lavender gingham dress.

I glanced around, looking for a car or a nearby dwelling – anything to explain her presence here, now. But there was nothing. Just the blooming yucca, the loom, and the woman, who had yet to acknowledge my presence.

I hesitated. I was pretty sure I was meant to talk to her – I mean, why else would the glowing thread and that crazy spider have rushed me all the way out here, and then disappeared? But then why hadn't she acknowledged my presence? She must have heard me; I hadn't been attempting to be quiet, hot and tired and thirsty as I was.

Thirsty. Just thinking of the word glued my tongue to the roof of my mouth. I slid my backpack off my shoulders and reached inside for a bottle of water. I had three bottles left, besides the partially empty one in my hand; I hadn't yet made it to my goal, wherever that was, and I would have to get back to civilization on foot. Not a comfortable situation to be in.

I looked at the old woman working the loom in the desert sun. I looked at my water rations again. Then I took a small swig of water from the bottle in my hand and replaced it in the pack, brought out one of the full bottles, and approached the woman at the loom.

When I was closer, but still a respectful distance away, I said quietly, "*Yá'át'ééh abiní, amá sání.* I bring you water." Then I set down the bottle and stepped back to wait.

Don't ask me where I learned how to say, "Good morning, Grandmother," in Navajo. I'd probably stumbled across it online while looking up something else. And I was sure I'd butchered the pronunciation; Navajo is a tonal language, like some Asian languages, and very much not like English. The gods alone knew what I'd actually said. *My hovercraft is full of eels*, maybe.

Without turning, the woman reached down for the bottle, uncapped it, and took a sip. "*Ahéhee',*" she said – or rather, She said. For at last, I had put two and two together: the loom, the old woman, my arachnid guide. Emboldened, I stepped closer to inspect Her work. "You have let a flaw creep in here," I said, pointing to a spot in the design that didn't quite match the corresponding design on the opposite side of the otherwise symmetrical rug.

"Not a flaw," She said in perfect English, and squinted up at me. "As you well know, grandson."

I did know. She was Spider Woman, who had taught weaving to the Diné. You might say we were fellow fiber artists.

"How did You come here?" I asked, my voice low, as if the other gods might find us and whisk Her away again. Which they might, for all I knew. I still didn't have a clear picture of what was going on in the gods' world. "How did You get free?"

"Loki can't watch all of the exits all of the time," She said complacently, intent on Her craft.

I blinked. "Is there an entrance near here?"

"Yes, of course," She said. "You passed it on your way down."

"I did?"

"Well, you were close. But see here, grandson, I don't have all day. Attend!"

Burning with unanswered questions, I stepped close to Her left side and watched as She slid the ball of yarn through the warp strings for the middle of a pattern row. Knitting was more my thing, but I'd played with a loom a time or two, and I had taken a symposium on Navajo rug design in college. I could already tell Her rug would be in the Ganado style, or maybe Klagetoh. "What motif are You planning for the center?" I asked, as if chatting with a fellow enthusiast.

She turned ageless eyes on me and regarded me severely. "That is entirely up to you."

Daylight dawned once more. I stared at the rug as She swapped balls for a different color of yarn and went back to Her weaving. Then I collected myself. As She had said, we didn't have all day. "Grandmother," I said, "some very bad rumors are being spread about my mother. The rumors are meant to discredit her and make it more difficult for her to forge another peace agreement amongst the gods. I've come here to find the source of the rumors – a place where videotapes or computer memory chips might have been stored."

"I know of your errand," She said, still concentrating on Her work, "and I know the place you speak of. You are very close – it's just over the next rise. But attend, grandson." She beckoned me close with a crooked finger. Obediently, I bent toward Her as She spoke just above a whisper. "The man you seek is no longer sane. And his loyalty has once again been stolen by those who do not deserve it." She shook Her head. "He is a sad case, grandson, but you cannot save him. Don't even try. He is too far gone. And" – here She looked me over skeptically – "I'm not sure you have enough power to defeat the men he's helping. Their protector is strong, and no longer under Our control." Her brow lowered as She clenched Her ball of yarn so tightly that Her knuckles turned white.

That didn't sound encouraging. "Who is their protector?"

She shook Her head. "I've helped you as much as I dare. Go now. The compound is unguarded; the bad men had business in Shiprock. Just…be careful. And always, always leave yourself a lifeline." She gestured to Her right, and the gossamer thread reappeared.

"*Ahéhee'*," I said as I scooted around Her toward the path. "Thank You. For everything."

She regarded me with a kind smile. "Blood Clot Boy said you were a special young man. I should have believed Him."

I returned Her smile weakly. The Ute god had been allied with my great-grandfather, Looks Far Guzmán. Grandfather had been dead for fifteen years, but even now, whenever I thought of him, it felt like I'd been punched in the gut. "Please give Blood Clot Boy my regards, and tell Him I appreciate the compliment," I said.

"I will." She retrieved the water bottle from the rocky soil next to Her feet and tossed it to me. "Here. You'll need this."

I caught it one-handed and slid it back into my pack. Then I waved my thanks and headed out in the direction She had indicated.

About halfway down the hill, I turned around. As I'd expected, Spider Woman and Her loom were gone. "People come and go so quickly here," I muttered, and snorted at my own joke. This whole adventure did seem as surreal as Alice in Wonderland. At least nobody had ordered their guards to take off my head.

Yet.

I turned back to the shimmering strand.

Spider Woman had been right, of course. About a quarter-mile farther on, the shining thread joined with the bank of a dry wash and began to parallel it. Another quarter-mile and over a rise, I came within sight of an ancient RV.

The vehicle wasn't going anywhere; the tires were flat and probably long since rotted out. It was a good-sized unit – certainly large enough for someone to live in full-time, if they didn't have much stuff. It might once have had a paint job, or at least the manufacturers' logo on the side, but all of that had been scoured away by wind and sand, and bleached away by the sun.

A couple of outbuildings sat apart from the RV. One, I assumed by its size and smell, was an outhouse. The other, though, was much newer; made of corrugated steel, it looked like the kind of structure people used to house their motorboats and other expensive toys. A thick power line ran from an array of solar panels to the side of the building, and a satellite dish was mounted on the roof.

The place felt deserted, but I wanted to be sure before I started poking around. So I strolled up to the door of the RV and knocked, as if I were going next door to borrow a cup of sugar. "Hello! Anybody home?" I called out in a friendly voice. Hearing nothing, I tried the door handle; it opened easily. That the door was unlocked made sense to me. Who would come all the way out here to break into a derelict RV? Especially when it was clear that the good stuff, if there was any here, would be locked up in the pole barn.

Inside the RV, it was dark and smelly. Whoever lived there had put up blackout curtains over all of the tiny windows. My phone's flashlight app revealed a midden heap – piles of food wrappers, cans, and papers on every level surface, through which wound a path from the door to the sink and fridge, and from there to the bed in the back of the unit.

Something pinned to the curtain above the sink caught my eye. I moved closer, careful to avoid knocking over some pile that would block my retreat. "Oh, man," I breathed, when I saw it clearly at last. I recognized it immediately: it was a yellowed newspaper photo of my mother on the stage of the Greek amphitheater in Denver on the day the gods came back.

There was nothing else hung on any of the walls. Just the curtains, and that thirty-five-year-old photo of Mom.

I was beginning to get an inkling of just how crazy Jack Rivers had become.

I couldn't get out of the place fast enough. I forced myself to make a cursory check of the bedroom from the doorway, just to say I'd been over the whole place. Then I made my way as rapidly as I could through the trash piles until I could get the door open and taste fresh air again.

The compound was still empty of people when I got outside. Still, I hurried, crouching like a thief, to a spot behind the pole barn, where I dropped to my knees and concentrated on getting my breathing back under control.

When I could take in a breath without gasping – and when I could see something in my mind's eye other than that photo of Mom – I regarded the pole barn. Someone other than Jack Rivers had built it; I was sure of that. I had initially assumed Rivers would have stored everything on digital files – and probably not in cloud storage. Aunt Shannon had once observed, offhanded, that obsessive people would have multiple backups of everything, including five years' worth of grocery receipts – but the paranoid would stick to one or two copies and keep them on a non-network hard drive, because the only way to make sure something couldn't be hacked was to keep it totally out of reach of hackers.

So I assumed Rivers would have a couple of computers: one to access the internet and one that never went online, which he would use for storing all his files, together with external hard drives or maybe USB drives as his backup. I figured he'd keep it all in the RV – and maybe he had, until these guys arrived and built the pole barn.

I was in luck: not only did the structure have doors on either end, but the sliding door on this side didn't appear to be locked. I frowned at that. Why hadn't the interlopers locked the doors? Maybe they didn't think they had anything worth stealing? Fat chance. Maybe they didn't think anyone would track them down?

Maybe they thought they had better protection than a puny lock would provide?

That idea gave me pause. I realized that if I were in a movie, this would be the instant where the audience would be yelling at me not to go into the barn.

Of course, just like in the movies, I slid open the door and slipped inside.

Whoever they were, they had kitted out the place. On one side were a couple of cots, a fridge, and a hot plate. Next to the hot plate, and looking out of place, was one of those plastic water-on-demand stands you see in doctor's offices. The five-gallon water jug upended in the stand was close to empty, and only one sealed jug sat behind it. Now I knew the errand these guys had gone out on; five gallons of water wouldn't last long with three people using it.

Opposite the living area was a cluster of folding tables supporting several computers. Pay dirt! I stepped around a plastic crate and moved closer to inspect the setup. One computer appeared to be devoted to video production; I suspected this was the machine that had created the horrible video of Mom. I sat down and delved into the machine's history. Sure enough, it indicated a couple of external drives on which the raw video had been stored.

My eyes fell on an open shoebox that sat on the table amid a rat's nest of cords. Inside the shoebox was a jumble of old-fashioned memory chips, USB drives, and DVD cases. "It couldn't be that easy," I muttered, but that shoebox appeared to be the only place where any removable media were stored. I checked all the computers for additional chips and disks, tossing any I found in the box. Then I initiated a disk wipe on each machine. While I waited, I pulled some twine from a pocket with the intent of fashioning a carryall for the shoebox, as it wouldn't fit in my pack.

That's when I heard the groan.

It seemed to come from the far corner of the building, where the light from the work area didn't reach. I advanced cautiously, my left hand automatically reaching for the garrote I kept in a pocket on that side. I might not have laser eyes like my sister's, but I wasn't entirely defenseless.

"Water," the voice croaked. And then it said, "Joseph? Is that you?"

I flicked on my phone flashlight. There was a cage in the corner – the kind people use as kennels for big dogs – and inside the cage was an old man, cringing away from the sudden light. His hair was snow-white and he was thin to the point of emaciation. "Jack?" I said, in as close an approximation of my father's voice as I could manage.

"You've gotta get me out of here, Joseph," the man said, squinting. "Those bastards locked me in here when they left, but they didn't leave me any water."

"Who are they?" I asked, as I pocketed my phone and pulled a partially-empty bottle from my pack. "Which god are they working with? Is it Tezcatlipoca?"

I crouched beside the crate and handed the bottle through the bars. His hand shot out and clamped around my wrist like a vise. Surprised, I dropped the bottle; it rolled to a stop against the wall of the dog crate. "You're not Joseph," he growled, his face inches from mine. I could see the madness in his eyes and in the rictus of his scowl, and suddenly the wire mesh crate seemed a flimsy barrier, too easy to breach.

"You're right," I admitted, swallowing the sudden rush of fear. "But Joseph and Naomi sent me."

"Who are you?" he demanded.

"I won't tell you," I said. "Not until you tell me what's going on here."

He laughed, and tried to spit in my face. "*¡Cabrón! ¡Pendejo!* You don't know who you're dealing with!"

I twisted my arm and managed to break his grip. He laughed again and scooped up the water bottle, draining it in a single gulp. "You and that *tortuga* over there – you're cowboys. *Muy muy.*" He spat again. "Just wait 'til the other guys get back, and we'll see how tough you are."

"*¿Tortuga?*" Turtle? I glanced around. The only thing I saw was the plastic crate I'd bypassed on the way to the computer – and a tiny, glowing spider bouncing around on top of it. "Oh, gods." The spider hopped to my shoulder as I flipped open the crate. It appeared to be full of sand, but I stuck my hand down in it, and almost immediately hit something that felt very much like a shell. "Crap," I said, and broke for the full five-gallon jug of water. I rolled it into position, opened it swiftly, and began dumping the contents into the crate.

Kappas are water creatures – if they can't be in it, they have to carry it around with them in a concavity on the tops of their heads. If they lose that somehow, they're paralyzed. I assumed Rivers' comrades had trapped Enkou by getting him to dump the water out of his head; it was easy to do, and I knew Loki knew the trick because I'd seen Him do it to Enkou once before. Throwing the kappa in sand, I guessed, was a precaution – like the ancient trick of drying out your phone by sticking it in a bag of rice. But it served my purposes, too – or at least, I hoped the wet sand would be enough to bring Enkou around. Although if I meant to get him home – and I did – I'd still need water for the top of his head. Now that Jack Rivers had my partial bottle of water, I had only one full bottle left. We'd have to be very careful going back across the desert.

Or, hey, we could steal the bad guys' truck. Which I could hear even now, in the distance, roaring toward us with a backfire that sounded like farting.

As the back door slid open, Rivers began to laugh – a low, menacing sound. "You're fucked, *pendejo*," he said gleefully.

"No, Jack," my father said, stepping into the barn. "*You're* the one who's fucked. Again."

"Joseph!" Rivers whined, on his knees now, his fingers laced through the mesh side of the cage. "You've gotta get me out of here!"

"Not a fucking chance," Dad snarled as he stepped toward the cage. "What made you think it would be a good idea to go up against

Naomi and me again, huh? You and I had a deal! If you left us alone, we'd leave you alone! But if you messed with us again, your ass would be *mine*."

I had never seen my father so full of righteous rage as he was at that moment, towering over the cage in which Jack Rivers cowered, as far away from Dad's looming figure as he could get. "He came to me in a dream," Rivers babbled. "He said he'd smother me if I didn't help. Then he was all in my lungs – I couldn't *breathe*, Joseph!" He scratched at his own throat, drawing blood. "I *had* to say I'd help!"

At the word *smother*, I could only stare at the man. I'd felt smothered by the smoke monster in my own dream.

The light from the back door was blocked for a moment as Uncle George filled the opening. "Joseph, we need to get a move on. Oh, hey, Webb. How's it going?"

I lowered the empty water jug to the floor and grabbed the shoebox. "I'm good," I said, hooking my backpack over one shoulder. "But we need to take the crate. Enkou's in it."

My father and my uncle stared at the crate. The sand inside was beginning to shift. "What's *he* doing here?" Uncle George said.

"The same thing I am, presumably," I said. "Let's go."

The sun was low in the western sky as we exited the pole barn and ran to Uncle George's hovercar, which was parked beside a solar panel about a hundred yards away. Dad and Uncle George carried the crate between them. "Jesus, this thing is heavy," Uncle George complained. "You think the car will fly with all this weight in it?"

"It'll be fine," said Dad, as they hefted the crate into the back of the car. "Get in."

I heard shouting, and turned. The guys in the truck had spotted us and were now headed in our direction, kicking up a plume of dust as their vehicle roared over the uneven ground.

"Webb!" Dad yelled. I sprinted to the back door and threw myself inside just as Uncle George lifted off.

The truck changed course again, backfiring all the way – and now I saw one of the guys poke an arm out of the window. "Dad?" I said, just as the guy began shooting at us.

"Oh, nice," muttered Uncle George. "I'm just about out of lift. Hey Enkou, we could use a little help here."

I flipped my head to gaze at the back of the car, where Enkou's head stuck up from the crate. He blinked slowly, swiveled his head, and then drew a paw out of the muck to point to the east.

Uncle George grinned. "I love it when a plan comes together," he said, and steered our hovercar so that it flew directly over the wash. The guys in the truck followed us into the dry creek bed.

No more than a minute later, a wall of water came barreling down the wash. In moments, the driver of the truck had lost control, and the truck floated away.

"That pole barn's gonna flood," Uncle George said conversationally. Sure enough, I heard a boom of – thunder? No. It was the water coming in contact with the electronic equipment in the pole barn. We circled back to see the devastation. Rivers' RV was parked high enough up the rise to be unaffected, but the rest of the site was under a good couple of feet of water. The solar panels had been knocked every which way. And the pole barn itself was a total loss – both doors had blown off, and scorch marks showed above the front door.

"What about Jack?" Uncle George asked quietly.

"What about him?" Dad said. I went cold all over at his tone.

"Do you think he got out?"

"That fucker has more lives than a cat," Dad said. "Of course he got out. Somebody probably rescued him."

I saw no sign of a floating dog crate. Of course, the gods could have just snatched him up and left the crate behind. But I suspected – and clearly Dad was hoping – that the gods had had their fill of Jack Rivers and, having used him up, had abandoned him at last.

"Need anything from your car?" Dad asked me as we flew away from the site.

"No, I grabbed all the important stuff. How did you know to come after me, anyway?"

"A rancher spotted the wreck when he went out to check on his herd," Dad said. "He reported the license tag to the state police, and they called Hilary, who called your mother and me."

"Oh, gods," I said faintly, picturing my girlfriend in a panic. "I never called her after I rolled the car. I told her I'd be home by dinnertime tonight."

Uncle George craned his neck westward, where the sun was heading for the horizon. "Looks like you'll be a little late."

"Yeah, but not as late as I could have been," I said. "Thanks for coming after me. And thanks for arriving in the nick of time, too." I pulled the last water bottle from my bag and turned around to take care of Enkou. With his head cavity filled, he climbed out of the crate and clambered over the back of the seat to plop down beside me. "I don't know how I would have gotten Enkou out of there if it hadn't been for you guys."

The ninja turtle patted my knee. "You good man," he said. "Would have found way."

"What were you doing down there, anyway?" I asked, trying not to sound like I was scolding him, even though I was. "Hilary has been worried sick about you."

"Sorry," he said. "Had job. Fill metal house with water."

I didn't bother to ask him who had told him to do it; experience had taught me I wouldn't get a straight answer out of him, no matter how hard I tried. Instead, I pulled out my phone and called Hilary. I figured once she started to bitch me out for worrying her, I'd just hand the phone over to Enkou. She'd be so grateful that I'd found him that she'd forget all about being mad at me.

## While Webb was calming Hilary down...

I was doing my best to settle into life in the Neo-Atheists' camp. Truly, I was. But most days, it was all I could do to keep from slapping someone. Or, alternately, frying something with my eyes out of sheer boredom.

The National Neo-Atheists Movement basically believed life had reached its zenith in America a hundred years back, in the 1950s. Men were the breadwinners; they did all the important work and made all the important decisions. The little woman was supposed to stay home to cook, clean, and care for the children. A sparkling house and well-behaved children were the highest achievements women could attain, and any woman who fell short – well, her husband had the right to discipline her any way he thought best.

It was difficult to clean everything to a shine when you were living in a tent, so that part had fallen by the wayside – at least for now. Once the movement grew and we could live in the open, our founder assured us, women would be held to the same high standards as men were. Just, you know, our tasks were different, and required less brainpower. For which we were supposed to be thankful, because, hey, our men were taking care of us. We didn't have to worry our pretty little heads about anything any more. And so on.

This movement had quite a bit of growing to do before it could take over America. Including Rafe and me, just seven couples lived in the compound. The living quarters were platform tents that leaked when it rained; I spent a large part of my day drying out our clothes and bedding. There was a bathhouse with a laundry tub, but no running water. I brought buckets of water up from the stream, heated them over a fire, and scrubbed our clothing clean by hand, just as the rest of the women did when it was their laundry day.

And while we women toiled without modern conveniences, the men worked in relative comfort in an abandoned cabin they had rescued from the forest.

None of the couples had children, which I privately considered to be a blessing – but as almost everyone here was in their twenties, I knew that was just a matter of time.

Faith in God had been a big part of life in 1950s America, but the men of the National Neo-Atheists Movement rejected religion. A lot had happened since 1955 – the gods had come back, and as it turned out, most of Them didn't have any patience for the line of crap these guys were spouting. So the Neo-Atheists' creed was that the "gods" were fakes, probably dreamed up by liberals and Native Americans to strip white men of their rightful place in society. If these men believed in a god at all, it was Jehovah – and not the post-Second-Coming Jehovah, either. But most didn't believe in any god, and knew better to admit to it if they did.

In any case, everyone had to live by the movement's code of ethics:

1. Any man who professes a belief in the gods is an enemy.
2. Any man who believes the "gods" that arrived in the so-called Second Coming are fakes is a friend.
3. No man shall allow his wife to dress immodestly.
4. No man shall sleep with another man's wife.
5. No man shall drink alcohol.
6. No man shall kill any other man.
7. All men are equal.

You might recognize the code. The founders lifted it, with minimal tweaking, from George Orwell's *Animal Farm*. And just like in the novel, it hadn't taken long for the society to begin to break down.

The wives all knew. We talked about it in hushed tones when we gathered for our coffee klatches and quilting bees. "There's a still in the woods," Miriam Jones said one day during my very first week there, as we bent over our handiwork. I'd never been much of one for crafts – I'd left that to Webb – but I could sew a seam by hand, and that appeared to be most of what quilting required.

"How do you know?" asked Tansy Longmire.

"Randy came home smelling like a brewery the other night," Miriam said. "I asked him about it while he was still drunk enough that he didn't care what he said." She gave us a small smile.

"Frank has come home smelling of alcohol a time or two, as well," said Elvy Johnson. "I never thought to question him about it while he was still drunk. That was smart of you, Miriam."

Miriam shrugged and went back to work.

"I don't dare ask Truro anything when he's been drinking," Agnes Barnstead said, unconsciously fingering the black-and-yellow skin around her left eye. Agnes and Truro were Ducky's former parishioners, and I had already had enough conversations with Agnes to know that leaving Chicago for this little slice of heaven had totally been Truro's idea. I had been really concerned for her well-being the first time I met her, when the bruise was fresh. But she had waved me off, saying that if Truro thought she deserved a smack, well, then, she probably did. It was all I could do not to knock both their heads together.

At another get-together that week, I discovered Agnes had more to worry about than physical abuse. She had just excused herself to go the privy; as soon as she was out of earshot, Emmy Proffitt said, "Poor thing. She doesn't know, does she?"

"What doesn't she know?" I asked.

"Why, that Truro's sleeping with Tansy Longmire," Emmy said, and sighed. "It will be so hard for her when she finds out she's sharing her man with another woman."

"It's always hard the first time," Elvy Johnson said.

I pretended to be aghast. "The first time?" I said. "You mean all the men sleep around? But it's in the code!"

The other women all nodded, and some of them gave me pitying looks. "You'll see, soon enough," Emmy said. "One of these days, we'll be gossiping about Ted and one of us. Maybe it'll be me." She gave me a come-hither look, batting her eyelashes at me as the other women laughed.

I couldn't join in the fun – not even for the sake of the mission. "Ted and I have a very solid relationship," I said. "He doesn't need any other woman but me."

Emmy met my level gaze and said, "We'll just see about that, won't we?"

Elvy, who was a bit older than the rest of the women in our group, broke the brief silence that followed. "You're a good-looking woman, Gemma," she said, a touch of envy in her voice. "I'm surprised none of the men have slept with *you* yet."

I gave her an arch look. "Ask me no questions and I'll tell you no lies," I said, earning admiring exclamations from most of the other women. "But really," I said, "if one of the other men wants to…you know…with you, what do you do?"

Elvy looked at me as if I'd grown another head. "You submit, of course."

"What?"

"What else would you do?" said Agnes, who had returned from the privy. She looked around the circle. "He's a man. What other choice do we have?"

"I don't know," I said slowly.

Agnes raised her hand to her cheek once more. "You try not submitting when a man wants sex, and let me know how that turns out for you."

"Say!" Tansy said brightly. "We're almost done with the quilt we've been working on. We should talk about what we want to tackle next. Maybe a double-sized quilt for our new friends Ted and Gemma. What do you say, ladies?"

And the conversation turned on its heel as the women began peppering me with questions about Ted's favorite color and the kinds of quilt designs I was partial to.

Even as I responded, I kept glancing at Emmy – and every time I did, she was glaring at me. I was pretty sure my big mouth and I had made an enemy of her. Which was unfortunate, as she was Ward Proffitt's wife.

At dinnertime, Ted and I would talk and laugh about how we had spent our day. I would play the perfect housewife, serving up whatever the other wives and I were cooking in the communal kitchen – really a fold-up camp kitchen, repurposed from some Boy Scout unit, and a two-burner propane stove – and listen while he joked about the guys at the office.

Later, snuggled into our sleeping bags against the increasingly chilly nights, Rafe and I would exchange our more important intelligence in whispers. Rafe already knew much of what I'd learned – juicy gossip to the wives was apparently the stuff of bragging rights for the men. His information was more substantial. Ward Proffitt was not just the titular head of the group; he was, in fact, the founder. Douglas Smith and Robert Jones, the two men who had escorted us from Greenville, were Proffitt's second-in-command and security detail. Rafe was pretty sure they were operating under assumed names. But then again, so were we.

The rest of the men appeared to be honest-to-goodness recruits, although none of them were particularly forthcoming about what had prompted them to join. Rafe was working most closely with Jake Longmire, the group's webmaster. Frank Johnson's title was outreach coordinator. He spent long days hunched over a computer, typing furiously and muttering to himself. Rafe would sometimes walk behind Frank's work station to get to the outhouse, and would cast a casual glance at his computer screen as he passed. Frank always seemed to be on some rabid anti-god website. "Probably posting screeds and looking for people to bring into the fold," he said.

That left Truro Barnstead, Ducky's former parishioner. Rafe couldn't tell what he was in charge of, other than operating the still. And fucking all the wives while beating up on his own.

At the end of our first week, more or less, Rafe told me about an offhand comment Proffitt had made about a prank he'd pulled in high school. "He said he tried to fry a turtle, and his girlfriend got mad at him," Rafe said.

"Why'd she get mad?"

"She told him to leave it alone because it was her turtle. Except he said she called it something else."

That got my attention. "A kappa?"

"He didn't say. And I didn't want to ask him, and get the guys to start asking me questions."

"Well, lots of people know what a kappa is now," I said. I didn't have to add that it was because of his climate change project.

"Yeah." Rafe was silent for a moment. "I wonder if he dropped that comment to test me."

Cold realization swept over me. "You think he's on to us?"

Rafe put a finger to my lips for a moment, reminding me that only a sheet of canvas stretched between us and any eavesdroppers. Then he said, "That we're animal lovers?"

I played along. "You think that would be a problem here?"

"I don't know, but let's not give them any reason to throw us out."

Number three on the code of ethics – the thing about the men not allowing their women to dress immodestly – was a pain in the ass, as far as I was concerned. And of course, it was the one that got me into trouble.

It was the start of our second week in the compound, and I'd had just about enough of wifely togetherness. What set me off was an incident the day before, when I walked in on the other wives whispering and giggling over something. Tina Smith, who was usually as quiet as a mouse, seemed to be in the middle of it. She had tucked her chin to her chest to hide her reddened face as she stitched furiously, making an uneven mess of her seam. And they all shut up as soon as they saw me.

I sat down and brandished a pair of scissors, which caused some of the ladies to gasp a bit theatrically. "Okay," I said, "out with it. Clearly, you've got some gossip involving Tina. Let's hear it."

Emmy Proffitt looked me in the eye. "You want to hear it? Fine. Ted's sleeping with Tina."

My initial reaction was to turn on my laser eyes and fry them all on the spot. But I schooled my features to impassiveness while I thought about which reaction would further our mission. Then my eyes fell on Tina again, and I realized she wasn't just embarrassed – she was crying.

"I'm so sorry, Gemma," she said, nearly sobbing. "I didn't want to. I knew you'd be hurt."

If I'd had any doubt that Emmy had lied, Tina's reaction dispelled it. "It's all right," I found myself saying automatically. I even handed her a tissue. "I guess that's just the way it is here, huh?"

She rushed to hug me so quickly that her handiwork dumped from her lap into the dirt. "Thank you for understanding," Tina said as I hugged her – as if she had been the only victim.

That afternoon – after helping to make lunch for the men and cleaning up – I begged off the wives' sewing circle, pleading a headache. Most of the women made sympathetic noises, although Tina looked miserable and Emmy looked triumphant.

I did retire to my tent, but about a half-hour later, I slipped out for a solo walk in the woods.

It was a beautiful day for a walk, too. The air was crisp, the sky was blue, and the leaves were nearing their peak. I grew up with gold-and-green autumns – aspen, birch, and evergreen – so even after living in Virginia for many years, the reds and browns of Eastern trees still surprised and pleased me.

When I reached a rushing brook, I sat down with my back against a tree and thought about what my next move should be. The obvious one would be to talk to Rafe – but I couldn't do it here. I was too pissed off at him. What if I blew up at him, which I had no doubt I would, and the group disciplined us – me for my insubordination and him for not keeping his wife under control?

And then I had an ugly thought. He had said he'd fucked Tina only as part of the job, and I'd accepted that. I knew the men were supposed to sleep around. The wives had talked about it like it was a hazing ritual. You're not really part of the inner circle until you've sampled all the women, or something. But then I thought about my conversation with Rafe on the drive down here, and wondered whether he'd wanted to have sex with her. Tina was certainly quiet and submissive. She'd never be critical of Rafe.

Then again, maybe he picked her because she was so quiet – and therefore, perhaps, the least likely to carry the tale back to me. Although if that was his reasoning, he hadn't been paying enough attention to what I'd said about the group of wives being a viper's nest.

And why would he be interested in another woman now? I'd spent the last week and a half being submissive and dutiful. I hadn't criticized him once, that I could think of. If that's what he wanted, then I was giving it to him. Why sleep with someone else?

Round and round my thoughts went, like an ouroboros of dismay and wounded pride. I wasn't conscious of how much time had passed until I realized I had to pee. It was a long way back to the bathhouse – the only approved place in the compound where a woman could undress, other than her tent – and I honestly didn't think I could hold it that long. So I stepped into the woods several hundred yards away from the stream, pulled down my undies, squatted, and let go.

Too late, I heard someone moving through the fallen leaves. "Well, isn't that a pretty picture," said Truro Barnstead as he stepped into view from behind me. "You're not supposed to go around unclothed, you know. Somebody might get the wrong idea."

"Sorry," I said, dropping my eyes and reaching for my panties. "I didn't think I could make it back to camp. I didn't see the harm."

"You can just leave those panties right where they are," he said, pushing my shoulder so that I tipped over onto my side. "Our ethical code is there for a reason, you know. I've a mind to teach you a lesson."

"Did you follow me?" I said, curled onto my side, as I fought to keep my dress down.

"Of course I did," he said, deftly slipping my panties off my feet. The smell of rotgut liquor wafted from him. "You want to do it doggie-style? Sure thing, honey." And he pulled me up onto my knees while he penetrated me from behind, his hands cupped around my breasts.

I couldn't help it. I was already mad at Rafe, or hurt or something, and now this drunken sot was raping me? I trained my eyes on the back of his right hand and let fly.

"Ow! Jesus, that hurts!" He pulled out and scampered back, staring at his reddened hand. "What the fuck did you do to me?"

"I taught you a lesson," I said, still angry. "I'm not as defenseless as Agnes. And if you're smart, you won't tell anyone what just happened here, or I'm liable to show you what else I can do."

"Bitch!" he screamed. "Stupid fucking whore!" Then he stumbled off into the woods, shouting, "You'll pay for this!"

"Well, that went well," I said under my breath, as I shook the leaf mold out of my panties. I considered not going back to the camp at all, but that would leave Rafe alone to face the consequences of my actions. And I didn't have it in me to do that. Whatever the truth behind what he'd done with Tina, I still loved the guy.

Supper that night was uncomfortable. Truro wore a massive bandage wrapped around his right hand. "Burned it on the still," was his terse answer to anyone who asked him about it. But he glowered in my direction whenever he caught sight of me – and others noticed.

*Thanks for fingering me, Captain Obvious.* I ignored him as I went on with my work.

That night, cocooned in our sleeping bag, Rafe said, "What did you do to Truro?"

"He raped me," I said.

"What?"

"So I burned his hand a little."

"Oh, gods," he breathed. "Are you trying to get us in trouble?"

"He. Raped. Me," I said, more distinctly, as Rafe tried to shush me. "Did you miss the part where I said he raped me?"

"They don't believe in rape," he said softly.

"Well, I do!"

"Be quiet!" he hissed. And then, at last, he heard what I'd said. "Oh, gods, Sage," he said, and pulled me into his arms.

That simple act brought my guard down. I sobbed against my husband's shoulder, and he held me until I cried myself out. "I can't wait to get out of here," I said when I could form coherent words again.

"Me neither," he said, and the way he was trembling, I knew he meant it.

"Can I ask you something?" I said, a few moments later. "Did you sleep with Tina?"

He let out a sigh – of relief or guilt, I couldn't quite tell. "Yeah. I was hoping you wouldn't find out."

I laughed bitterly. "Seriously? When everybody knows everybody else's business here, within two seconds of it happening?" And then I realized what I'd just said. "Shit. They're all gonna know what really happened to Truro."

"Yeah, they are." Clearly, he had already done the math.

We held each other silently for another few minutes. Then I said, "Did you want to?"

"Did I…?" I could almost hear him shifting gears in his head. "Oh. No, of course not. They were making a joke out of the fact that I hadn't screwed any of the women here but you. Then Robert basically handed me his wife and said, 'If you can't get it up for her, I'll understand. She just lays there for me.' And then he stood there and watched while…" He shuddered. "It was awful. I felt so sorry for her."

I couldn't process my feelings about that. "When was this?" I asked.

"Yesterday afternoon. Right before supper."

I remembered Tina rushing into the communal kitchen that afternoon, well after the rest of us had arrived. She had volunteered to chop the onions for the chili we were making that night – to mask her tears from her ordeal, I guessed now. "Poor thing. Poor both of you. Gods, but this is an awful place. Was society really like this before the Second Coming?"

He shook his head. "We'd gotten past all this. Mostly."

Then I thought of something else. "So we have about twenty-four hours before the shit hits the fan."

"That sounds about right," he said.

I began to weep again. "Shit," I hissed through my tears. "I don't think I can do this."

"You have to," he said, shaking me a little. "We both have to. We don't have a choice. Otherwise we'll ruin everything."

I nodded and wiped my nose with the back of my hand. He was right, of course. We'd had plenty of training in just this sort of emotional sleight-of-hand – stifling our true feelings in order to see a project through. But it was one thing to do it in training, and another to do it for real.

I wiped my eyes again and turned over. Rafe scooted over and spooned against my back. I let him do it, as we both needed the body heat.

Neither one of us slept much that night, wondering when the hammer would fall, and how – and whether we could get out with our lives. The ethics code said no man should kill another man, but that didn't mean this group would follow it any more closely than they honored anything else their laughable code called for.

We got a day of grace, as well as more information about the structure of the organization. Which was good, as it gave us something to talk about, other than the elephant in the room.

"This is only one cell," Rafe told me during our pillow-talk session Monday night. "There was another cell in the Southwestern desert somewhere, with a video production unit that was putting together material as part of Frank's outreach efforts. But it blew up last night."

"Blew up?"

"Well, not literally. You know how these guys are."

I didn't. At least not about hyperbole in the workplace. No women were allowed inside the cabin except for Emmy Proffitt, and she only went in to clean. Stifling my irritation at him, I asked, "So what actually happened?"

"Flash flood down an arroyo, from what I could tell," he said. "Took out the production facility and the solar array that was powering it. We had two guys there. Well, three. Two of them were in a truck that got washed downstream. They were rescued. These guys don't know what happened to the third guy, but they don't sound particularly upset about him being gone. Ward called him a crazy old coot."

"Nice. So supportive of a guy who might be dead." I shook my head. "You think we're the only remaining cell?"

"I don't know," he said, frustration creeping into his voice. "Ward talks big, like the association is nationwide. And supposedly they're setting up cells in other countries. But I can never pin him down on specifics, and Ward's files are all password-protected with an algo I've never seen before."

"Maybe Grady will be able to break in," I whispered. "We need to contact Darrell."

"Agreed," Rafe whispered back. "And Ward spent almost the whole day in conference with Frank. I think they were shooting a new video in response to what happened out west."

My irritation flared again. Rafe was getting so much more information than I ever could. Darrell shouldn't have sent me – my skills were useless here, and women were nothing but sex slaves. As soon as I thought the words *sex slaves*, tears pricked my eyelids. "I want to go home," I whispered, hating the whiny tone in my voice and hating myself for being so ineffective and weak. "If I have to keep this up much longer, I'm going to crack."

Rafe nodded decisively; I couldn't see it in the dark, but I felt his forehead graze mine. "Me, too," he said, his voice rough. Then he mastered himself. "Pack our stuff tomorrow. I'll message Darrell in the morning that he needs to pull us out."

## Chapter 9

Dad and Uncle George dropped off Enkou and me around eleven o'clock. Hilary was overjoyed to see Enkou; the kappa repaid her delight by snatching two cucumbers from her outstretched hands and making a beeline for our backyard pond.

"He's never been all that affectionate," she said, arms folded, as we stood on the deck and watched him paddle around. "Even that time when I rescued him from Ward, he didn't act happy about it."

"Maybe he wanted to drown Ward himself," Uncle George offered. "Some guys just don't like being rescued. It hurts their pride."

"He was certainly glad the cavalry showed up this time," I told her as we trooped back inside to the living room. "There was no way he was going to get out of that crate full of sand on his own."

She made a noise that sounded suspiciously like a harrumph. "Maybe he's mad I didn't come with."

"Screw him, then," I said, encircling her shoulders with my arms. "I'm glad you weren't there. It was no place for the mother of my child."

She whacked my chest with an outstretched palm. "I'm perfectly capable of taking care of myself, oh knight in shining armor." Then she lay her head against me. "I'm just glad y'all are both home safe."

Dad's phone chirped with the ringtone he used for Mom. He pulled it from his jeans pocket with a smile. "Hi, sweetheart. We're in Boulder, dropping off Webb." He tilted the phone down, away from his mouth. "Your mother says hi."

"Hi, Mom," Hilary and I chorused obediently.

He grinned. "You heard that?...How are you? No, really, how are you feeling?" His smile faded. "Okay. I know. Is Shannon with you?...Good. We'll see you in forty-five minutes, tops. I love you." He ended the call and stuffed the phone back in his pocket, and then turned to Uncle George. "Let's roll."

"Hell, yeah," he said. "I need to get to bed. Tomorrow's a working day, and the boss will be pissed at me if I'm late."

"Yes, he will," said the boss, his coyote grin back in place.

"Dad?" I said.

"Not now, Webster."

That was the last thing I wanted to hear on this weird and exhausting day. "Gods damn it!" I shouted. "Would one of you *please* tell me what's going on with Mom?"

That got Dad's attention; he knew I tried not to swear. He and Uncle George shared a guilty look. Then Dad put a hand on my shoulder. "Look, it's not fair. I know it's not fair. But she made me promise not to tell you. She wants to tell you herself."

"That's bullshit on her part, because she's had ample opportunity and it hasn't happened." I shrugged off his hand. "Come on, Dad. It's no secret that she's sick. But I'd like to know what we're dealing with. I deserve to know."

Dad had always had a knack for the stoic Indian look – strong, silent, and impassive – and he employed it now. Unfortunately for him, he'd passed the talent on to me.

It was Hilary who broke the stalemate. "She has cancer, doesn't she?"

His face fell.

My reality shifted. That made three – no, four – reality shifts that day, and I was out of resources to deal with them. "How is that even possible?" I howled.

I mean, it should have been impossible for my mother to have cancer. Most cancers had been eradicated not long after the Second Coming, when a select few pharmaceutical company CEOs and researchers received visits from the gods, who told them where their priorities would be directed henceforth.

"Nobody knows," Uncle George said, as Dad turned away. "Hers seems to be one of the ones that doesn't respond to treatment."

I looked back and forth between his face and my father's back. "What about Aunt Shannon…?"

"She's tried, Webb. She thinks she's got a handle on it, and then it comes back." His face began to crumple, too.

"She's…dying?" I groped behind me for the arm of the couch, and sat.

"She's got the best doctors," Dad said, still not turning around. "We're determined to beat it."

"But why hasn't the goddess helped her?" *Like Blood Clot Boy helped Grandfather? Like Coyote helps you?*

Dad just shook his head.

"We need to go," said Uncle George. "I'll make damn sure Naomi calls you in the morning."

"Okay," I said automatically. "Drive safely."

"Will do. Come on, Joseph." Uncle George clapped my father on the shoulder and led him out to the hovercar. I went to the door, with Hilary right behind me, and watched as they got into the car. Or rather, Uncle George got in; Dad opened the passenger side door, then stripped quickly, piled his clothes on the seat, and shifted into the form of an owl. Then he flew away, with Uncle George following him at a lower altitude.

I shut the door. "Dad's flying home," I said, although she'd seen as much as I had.

"I'm so sorry, honey," she said.

"I just don't get it," I said, running a hand through my hair. "How can she be sick? How can she be dying?"

"Nothing makes sense right now," Hilary said. "The gods are gone and your mom's sick. It's like the animals are running the zoo." She took my hand. "Come on. Let's go to bed. The world will still be crazy in the morning, but at least we'll have had some sleep."

"I'm not sure I'll be able to sleep," I said, allowing her to pull me toward the bedroom. But the past few rough nights had caught up with me; I was out almost before my head hit the pillow.

And for the first time in days, Hilary didn't have to shake me awake as she left for work. I woke up at my normal time, started the coffee, tossed a couple of cucumbers out the back door for Enkou, and took a shower. Then I settled myself on the couch with a mug of coffee, and slid into the timestream.

I wasn't sure what sorts of answers I expected to find. I already knew I was bound up somehow in the gods' battle, so the outcome of that was closed to me. And I was pretty sure I was too close to my mother's situation to find out whether she would survive. But maybe I could learn something about Sage and Rafe. Or Jack Rivers.

I surfaced from my own life and rose above it all – admiring, as always, the beauty of the arrangement, and complimenting myself on the simulation I'd invented. You see, time doesn't really move in a stream; it's more like a web, with everything interconnected and everything that could possibly happen existing at once. While it's an exaggeration to say that the movement of a butterfly's wing can affect events on the other side of the world, it's not outside the realm of possibility, if a number of other things coincidentally happen at the same time. Events could line up such that a butterfly could pluck the web in Laos, say, and someone would die of a heart attack in Ontario. Or fall in love in Argentina. Or be cured of cancer in Colorado. Or all of those things at once.

So while I couldn't see precisely whether my mother would survive, I might be able to trace events that intersected with her line but had nothing to do with me. And it was easier for me to see those connections if I visualized time as a stream instead of as a web. It might seem counterintuitive to you. But don't forget: I live backwards.

I began with Mom's line. To my relief, it didn't appear to wink out any time soon. I could see powerful events feeding into it – Aunt Shannon was definitely involved, and so was a deity. The timestream didn't typically show me which god or goddess was involved, but there were usually hints that helped me figure out who it was – particularly if I had personal knowledge of Him or Her. This time, I was stumped. I memorized a couple of key points about the stream so I'd recognize it if I ran into it again later, and moved on.

At one point, Mom's line sort of smeared out of focus, which meant my own actions would have a bearing on it, too. Curious.

I moved back along the line, to see whether I could tell when Mom got sick. All right, I admit it – I wanted to know how long she'd been holding out on Sage and me. But as I traced the line back, I noticed the unknown deity's line had intersected with hers before. Several times before, in fact. Did Mom have another goddess besides White Buffalo Calf Pipe Woman?

Or maybe it was a deity who was making her sick?

Why would a god bother to make my mother sick? Why, to foul up the mediation of a new power-sharing agreement, of course.

I wanted to discover more about this mystery god, but I knew Hilary would be up soon, and I needed to check on Sage. So I soared aloft, over the glowing river, until I saw my sister's timeline. As usual, it was braided tightly with Rafe's – although I noticed a couple of recent breaks that troubled me.

The attack came without warning. As I cruised toward Sage's timeline, it felt as if a hand grabbed me by the scruff of the neck and yanked on me hard. Before I knew it, I was immersed in Sage's timeline – whether I wanted to be or not.

I wasn't actually with her physically, nor were these events happening as I watched. It was more like I was seeing a movie of something that would happen in the future.

Rafe and my sister stood inside a log cabin. A couple of tough-looking guys flanked them on either side, and four men sat before them at a folding table, as if passing judgment on them. I could see my sister's eyes beginning to glow, which in my experience was never a good sign. Then one of the tough guys restrained Rafe while the other one tied a blindfold around Sage's head and pulled her, spread-eagle fashion, across the folding table. As one of the men at the table began loosening his belt, the place exploded in light.

I could have told them the blindfold wouldn't work.

I tried to ease myself out of the stream to get a better look at it from above; I had a sense that a number of lines converged here, and I wanted to see what might come of all this. And okay, I admit it – I was scared for Sage. I was desperate to know whether she really was going to be gang-raped while her husband watched, or whether there was a way out of it for them both.

But my tormentor had no intention of easing my concerns. Instead of rising gently up and out of the timeline, I shot out as if I'd been kicked out – and found myself within a cloud of smoke.

"You have played into my hands, little spider," the smoke monster said. "You and your family have crossed me too many times."

"What are you doing here?" I said, or thought I did, with fists clenched at my sides. "You can't be here! No one can! This is my own creation. It's impossible for anyone to be here but me."

The monster's chuckles echoed inside my head. "I am stronger than you know," it said. "Soon…we will meet again soon…and then you will know me, and I will laugh as you pray to your puny gods to save you!"

With that, I was thrown back into *now*.

I wrapped both trembling hands around my coffee cup and drank; it had gone cold, but I could not have arisen to refresh it at that moment if my life had depended on it.

I needed to figure out who that smoke monster was, and fast. Because it knew what was going on with Sage and Rafe – and I had a feeling it might be involved in my mother's illness, as well.

All that, and the grant application, too.

After Hilary left for work, I sat down in my studio and took stock. It was Monday morning, and the application was due by 5:00 p.m. local time Wednesday. The 3D printer was all ready to create the model of my project, so I went ahead and set it up, fussed with a few settings, and let 'er rip. Then I searched through the bins of raw materials on my shelves to find the yarn I wanted to use for the pennants, and started working on them.

I told myself I was doing the right thing by attending to these mechanical and largely mindless tasks. They all had to be done anyway, and working on them gave me time to think about that final question I was having so much trouble answering.

That was my story, anyway. What I really found myself thinking about was the gods' disappearance, my sister's predicament, and my mother's illness.

I refused to believe Mom would die. I knew it was inevitable – every living thing on Earth dies, sooner or later – but I couldn't believe this was her time. Not when her first grandchild was on the way. Not while she was still on the outs with Sage. And certainly not when it looked like some god was messing with her – a god who could be discovered, presumably, and somehow stopped.

I thought again about the signature of the deity who I'd sensed meddling in Mom's timeline. It wasn't White Buffalo Calf Pipe Woman – that, I knew for certain. And it wasn't Aunt Shannon's goddess Brighid, or Sage's goddess Cerridwen, or Hilary's goddess Benzaiten. I would have been relieved had it been Brighid; healing is one of Her specialties.

But no. It was definitely a goddess, and it was one I'd never run into before. Moreover, She was going to be hard to track down if I couldn't find a way into the gods' realm.

Which reminded me of Spider Woman's odd comment, that I had passed an entrance or portal on my way to meet Her. The Southwestern United States is home to numerous sites that are sacred to Native Americans, but the really special ones are often hidden in plain sight. No one would have suspected that my great-grandfather's wickiup was perched atop the Utes' portal to the gods' realm; people just thought he was a nice old shaman who made a living by presiding over authentic sweat lodges for tourists.

So maybe I was looking for a tourist destination? Something out in the open, and maybe even well-known, yet secretive. A cavern, maybe, but I hadn't driven past any on my way down.

Then again, the caverns under the meadow above Grandfather's place weren't exactly advertised. And the same could be said of the portal in the Tlingit village Rafe came from in Alaska; that one was masked by an unassuming door behind the stage in the village meeting house. People were in and out of there all the time, yet only a handful – including Rafe, his mother, and my family – knew of the secret entrance to another world.

Then again, Spider Woman had said I'd driven *near* it, not past it.

I'd finished making the pennants, so I set them aside while I searched the internet. In moments, I had my answer – and was kicking myself for not making the connection earlier. What's well-known, mystical, and located in southwest Colorado? Why, the Anasazi ruins.

Now all I had to do was figure out which one housed the portal – and decide what I was going to say to the gods when I got there.

Piece of cake.

My sister's situation was tougher. I wanted to get on a plane and rescue her, wherever she was, even though I knew she was more than capable of rescuing herself. At the very least, I wanted to be there with her in the aftermath. She had Rafe, sure, but she'd need all the emotional support she could get. And emotional support was sort of my specialty. After making stupid stuff out of yarn, that is.

Which reminded me about the grant app. Sighing, I pulled up the application again. I'd stared at it for a good five minutes, no words coming to me, when my phone buzzed.

"Hey, babe," I said.

"Have you seen the news?" Hilary asked harshly.

"What? No." I switched back to the browser and began scanning the headlines. "Oh, no." Another video had been posted by our friendly neighborhood Neo-Atheists.

"Yeah." Her voice dripped with disgust. "Go ahead and watch it. I'm calling Darrell."

"Wait. What? Why?" They couldn't have put together another video about Mom; all of the raw video was in the shoebox I'd stashed under our bed.

"Just watch it," she said. "I have to go."

"Hilary!" I cried, but she had already ended the call. With my stomach clenched in something close to dread, I clicked on the link.

It was T. Warden Proffitt's show, for sure. A U.S. flag, used as a backdrop, filled the part of the screen that his face didn't. He looked to be in his mid-thirties, with blond hair, the angular mien of an ascetic, and the gleam of a mad prophet in his blue eyes. His name and the name of his organization flashed across the bottom of the screen.

"Ladies and gentlemen of America," he intoned, "our organization is under attack. The media won't tell you about this grievous injustice, controlled as they are by those beings who claim to be gods. So I come to you now to inform you of a crime – an unprovoked attack that has destroyed one of our settlements located in the southwestern part of the United States. This attack left two of our comrades gravely injured. Another is still missing."

By now, I'd figured out what he was driving at. I snorted. Calling Rivers' antique RV and the Neo-Atheists' production facility a "settlement" was stretching the truth.

"But we know who is responsible for this unwarranted attack. And while the authorities may not go after the perpetrator, the Neo-Atheists' Movement *will* see justice done." The camera zoomed in slowly, until I could almost count the pores on Proffitt's pointy nose. "Naomi Witherspoon, mark me well: your days are numbered. I will destroy you and your family – starting with your daughter."

A rooster crowed. Then the video abruptly cut off.

*Starting with your daughter.* And I knew exactly how they were going to do it.

I also understood why Hilary was contacting Darrell. But that didn't mean the idea didn't scare me to death.

I called her back. "Hotaru," I pleaded when she picked up the phone, "don't do it. Please don't get involved. These guys – you don't know what they're capable of."

"Too late," she said, sounding calmer than when she'd first called. "I've already talked to Darrell. He's going to put me in touch with Ward as soon as he can."

I glanced at the 3D printer, which was still slowly building my model. "Come home," I said. "Don't make the call from work."

"Why? What difference does it make?"

"I want to be with you when you talk to him," I said. "And I can't leave the house right now. The printer is printing my model. I mean, it would probably be okay if I just let it do its thing, but…"

Her voice softened. "So you're definitely gonna apply for the grant? You're not gonna deep-six your project?"

"I can't," I said. "You were right. It's too late to come up with another idea, and this is our best chance at a stable life for the three of us."

"Okay," she said. "I'm glad. I'll see you soon."

"Okay," I echoed, and ended the call. There was no way I could concentrate on the grant application right now, so I looked online for information on a freak flash flood in northwestern New Mexico.

The news report, when I finally found it, told it just as I remembered it.

FARMINGTON, Oct. 16 – A search is underway for a man reported missing in a flood Sunday, the San Juan County Sheriff's Department said.

Sheriff's deputies rescued two other men whose truck was swept away by the flood waters. They were treated and released from the San Juan Regional Medical Center in Farmington.

A metal outbuilding, a solar array, and other electronic equipment were destroyed in the flood. The cause is under investigation.

"Treated and released" hardly equated with "gravely injured." So Ward Proffitt definitely was not above stretching the truth. Somehow, knowing that didn't make me feel better. Especially since Hilary was going to be talking to him before the day was over.

She came home at lunchtime. I made sandwiches, which we both nibbled at. Then we sat on the couch and waited for Darrell to call.

And waited.

All of which gave us plenty of time to talk. Hilary said Darrell's agency had a pretty good fix on where Proffitt's merry band was located. What he wanted Hilary to do was draw him out, to see if he would slip and give her information on who or what was behind the Neo-Atheists. But failing that, if she could keep the guy on the phone long enough for Darrell's tech crew to trace the call, they would be able to move in and extract Sage and Rafe as soon as possible.

"It's because the last line of the video was what Darrell called a credible threat," she said.

"That's what I'd call it, too," I said. Then I realized I hadn't heard from my parents, despite Uncle George's promise to make sure Mom called me. So I called them.

"Your mother's having a rough day," Dad said. He was talking to us from their bedroom; I could see their windows and closet door behind him. "She'd rather not come to the phone right now."

"Is it because of the new video, or because of the…?" I couldn't choke out the word.

"Both," he said.

"Well, if it helps, we're on it," I told him. "Hilary's working with Darrell's team. She's supposed to talk to this Proffitt nutjob sometime this afternoon." Hilary began to wave her hands and shake her head violently. "And I guess that's all I'm allowed to say about that right now."

Dad's lips quirked up. "I see. Well, keep me posted when you're allowed to say more."

As soon as I ended the call, Hilary pounced. "What part of *secret clearance* do you not understand?" she said, exasperated.

"The part where you should have mentioned it before I called my parents," I retorted. "Anyway, I don't think there's any harm done. Is there?"

She folded her arms and walked away from me.

I took that as a cue to check the 3D printer, which had stopped making noises while I was on the phone with Dad. The silence turned out to be good news: the printing was done. I spent a few minutes affixing the pennants to the model, and then carefully labeled it and slid it into the box. I'd wait until morning to put packing material around it and seal it up, but I went ahead and made the shipping label and taped it to the box lid.

As I was finishing that, I looked up to see Hilary standing in the doorway, arms still crossed. "I should have stayed at work," she said. "I could have gotten a bunch of stuff done, instead of sitting here at loose ends, arguing with you."

"Assuming you could have concentrated well enough to get anything done."

"Well, there is that." She advanced into the room, her head down. "I'm sorry I snapped at you."

"It's okay. And I'm sorry I spoke out of turn," I said. "I think we've both been under a fair amount of stress for the past few days. Let's blame it on that, okay?"

"Deal," she said, and nestled herself into my arms. "I love you, Webb."

"I love you, too, Hotaru."

If we hadn't been waiting for Darrell to call, things might have gotten interesting then. But we were, so they didn't.

Just before five o'clock, Hilary's phone rang. We both jumped. Then she answered it. "Hello? Oh, hi, Darrell. Yes, I'm ready. Go ahead." She glanced over at me, her eyes wide but resolute. I grabbed the hand that wasn't holding the phone to her ear, as much to comfort myself as to anchor her.

"Hello, Ward," she said. Of course, I could hear only one side of the conversation; she wasn't about to turn on the speakerphone. "You know who this is? It's Hilary Takahashi…Right. We dated in high school. Seems like a million years ago, doesn't it?" She laughed a little bit. "So how are you? We haven't talked in a long time and…" She stopped speaking rather abruptly; I got the sense he was telling her how little time he had for social calls just now. "I'm sorry. I get it. So you're in a relationship?…Oh! Married! Well, congratulations to you and – what's her name? Oh, right, Emmy…Oh, nothing really new here. I'm still in Colorado. Graduated from college and never went home…So you're still in Durham?…Oh, the mountains. Yes, they're lovely. Great place to raise kids. Y'all have any?…Oh, that's too bad…Where are you looking to move to?…Huh. I never would have pegged you for someone interested in living in Canada. Where at?…Ooh. Sounds mysterious…Well, that's good to hear…Oh yes, Enkou's fine, and thanks for asking." Then she paused for a long time, as the color drained from her face. "What?" she said faintly. "I don't know what you mean…" Then she put down the phone. "He hung up."

"What was that at the end?" I asked, still gripping her hand.

"He said he knew everything about me, Webb," she said in a small voice. "He knew about you, and about the baby. And he said to tell you that after Sage, you're next."

"Oh, gods," I said, and pulled her against me as she wept.

When her phone rang a moment later, I answered it. "Darrell? It's Webb."

"Good," he said, all business. "Tell Hilary she did a great job."

I raised my eyebrows in her direction; she nodded, sniffed, and wiped her eyes on her sleeve. "She's right here. Let me put you on speaker so you can tell her yourself," I said, and punched the button for audio only.

"Hilary, you were great," Darrell said. "We got a lock on the phone signal and we recorded the whole call." He snorted. "This Proffitt fellow really is an amateur. He didn't even try to mask his location. Anyway, we're moving in on him and we're getting Sage and Rafe out."

"What about us?" Hilary said. "I've put Webb in danger, and the baby, too." She gulped back more tears and shook her head. "This is why I didn't want to work for JAF-H/D in the first place. I never should have called you. I never should have offered to help."

"She has a point," I said, slipping my arm around her shoulders. "About the risk to us, I mean."

"Don't worry. I'm already on it," Darrell said. "We're setting up protection for the two of you right now. Although to be on the safe side, I want you both to stay put until I give you the all-clear. Once we have Proffitt in custody, you'll have nothing to worry about."

"Sure," I said, not bothering to mask my sarcasm. "Life will be a piece of cake then. Just you wait and see."

## While Webb was talking about cake...

It seemed like we'd had no sleep at all when, several hours before dawn, Ward and his enforcers strode into our tent. "Let's go," he said, kicking at our feet. "Up and at 'em."

"What's this about?" Rafe said as he peered at our uninvited guests.

"Ted? Honey?" I said, staying put.

"You can drop the fake names," Ward said. "We know who you are. Get moving. Now!"

I was still inclined to bluff – at least until we were in a clear space where Rafe and I could shift and fly away. But then I heard the click of a firearm hammer being cocked, and my stomach clenched. We exchanged a look, and then got up and pulled our coats on over our pajamas.

It was snowing lightly, and my wholly impractical stilettos kept wanting to slide out from under me on the leaf-strewn dirt path. Rafe slipped an arm around me to steady me. I appreciated the gesture, although it did nothing to warm my bare legs under the coat.

The forced march to the cabin was short, at least. The place was ablaze with light; I wondered whether the men had met there through the wee hours, deciding our fates while we slept.

I realized when we got inside that my speculation might have been correct. Jake, Frank, and Truro sat at a folding table, looking awfully alert for the hour. Truro had unbandaged his hand, and stared at me with unmitigated hatred. Ward took a seat at the end of the table nearest Truro. Rafe and I were directed to a spot near the windows; we were not given chairs, nor were Robert or Douglas, who stood on either side of us. *Either standing is part of our punishment, or they don't expect this to take long*, I sent to Rafe.

*I'd bet on the latter*, he sent back. I was pretty sure he was right.

Ward kicked things off. He cleared his throat and said, "You, Raphael Orloff and Sage Orloff, came to us under false pretenses. You claimed to be Theodore and Gemma Wodehouse, a couple who espoused our beliefs. We welcomed you into our fold as equals. Yet you have both violated our code of ethics.

"Raphael Orloff, you have violated Point Number Two by allowing your wife to dress immodestly. You have also violated Point Number Three by sleeping with another man's wife. And you have also violated Point Number Four by drinking alcohol."

*They know our real names, but they don't know we're spies,* I sent to Rafe, somewhat relieved. Our everyday cover that we were civilian Defense Department employees had apparently held firm.

"What's my punishment?" Rafe said aloud. "If I'm not allowed to have a say in front of this kangaroo court, I'd like to get this over with so I can go back to bed. Jake and I have a lot of work to do in the morning."

Ward held up a hand. "In time." Then he turned to me. "Sage Orloff, you have violated Point Number Three by dressing immodestly. Moreover – and this is a much more serious offense – when Truro Barnstead attempted to mete out the punishment for unchaste wives unto you, you fought him, injuring him grievously." He nodded to Truro, who brandished his injured hand. I was surprised at how quickly it had healed; I'd thought I'd given him a third-degree burn in my anger, but the blistering was gone and pink skin showed where the wound had been.

But I set that puzzle aside to marshal my defense. "He raped me!" I said. "I was urinating in the woods, alone. I had no idea he was stalking me. When he found me with my pants down, he used it as an excuse to rape me. That's your punishment? To sexually abuse your women until they have no fight left in them?"

"And now you're speaking out of turn," Ward said.

"You're damn right I'm speaking out of turn!" I said, fury stoking the fire behind my eyes. "You men are nothing but barbarians!"

"That's enough!" Ward said, standing and pounding the table for emphasis. "Your sentence, Sage Orloff, is to be suitably punished by every man here. And your sentence, Rafe Orloff, is to watch us do it, so you learn the proper methods for punishing a wayward spouse."

"*What?*" I shrieked.

"Bind her eyes so she can't burn us," Ward said. "Truro goes first, since he didn't get to finish what he started the other day."

Douglas grabbed me in a headlock and bound my wrists. Just before the blindfold blocked my vision, I glimpsed Truro Barnstead unbuckling his trousers, a look of malicious glee in his eyes. Then I was shoved forward until my thighs connected with the folding table. Someone – I assumed it was Robert – pushed my head down and pulled my nightgown up.

"No!" Rafe shouted – as much to me as to the rapists around me. But I was past reason, and nearly past thought. Red-hot beams of light shot from my eyes, burning easily through the blindfold, then through the table, and finally through the cabin's wooden floor.

The men were all clustered at my other end, so none of them noticed what I was doing until flames began shooting up from the floor. "What the fuck *is* she?" I heard one of them shout.

"Fly, Sage!" Rafe yelled, and I shifted. Men screamed and reared back as my body shrank, elongated, and sprouted feathery flames. Unhindered now, I shot aloft, sweeping the room with my eyes and meting out my own fiery brand of punishment upon every one of those so-called men. Then I lit up the ceiling, and while our attackers writhed on the floor, Rafe and I escaped through the hole I had burned through the roof.

Once outside, I followed Rafe's lead as he circled the compound to survey what we had wrought. At first I was confused. Why were there so many people below us? All the men had been inside the cabin – why were there more out here? And why were they wearing fatigues?

I was still berserk enough to want to fry anything with a penis, but seeing the fatigues cleared my head at last. *Did you get a call in to Darrell?* I sent to Rafe.

*Nope. These guys came all on their own.*

*Huh. Any idea why?*

Rafe left off circling the camp and began heading northeast. *Nope*, he said again. *But I'm sure he'll fill us in. In the meantime, what's say you and I blow this popcorn stand?*

*I am right behind you*, I said.

We didn't shift back until we had reached the balcony of our condo in Arlington, across the Potomac River from Washington, D.C. Then Rafe and I shed pajamas and thrift-store coats, and clung to each other in our own bedroom. Relieved at last of the need to hide our feelings, we both broke down in tears.

"I'm sorry," he kept saying, over and over, as he stroked my hair. Then he began to rub my back in slow circles. When he moved in for a kiss, I reeled away from him, off the bed, and stood.

"What the hell do you think you're doing?"

"I…"

I nodded, hands on hips – a naked Fury in all Her glory. "That's what I thought. You figured one good cry was all it would take, didn't you? A good cry and a good fucking, and we'd both be all better. Marriage saved."

"What the hell are you talking about?" he cried as he stood.

"This mission isn't going to be that easy to put behind us," I went on.

"Project," he spat, correcting me.

"Oh, fuck that," I said. "Fuck Darrell's soft-pedaling what we do. Fuck Darrell. In fact, fuck JAF-H/D. And fuck you, too."

I could almost see Raven behind Rafe's eyes, searching for the trick that would get him out of this. "Look, Sage, I said I'm sorry," he temporized. "What else do you want from me?"

"For starters, you need to get that" – I pointed at his flaccid penis – "tested for disease before I'll allow you to stick it in me again."

"Disease?" he hooted. He threw his hands in the air and walked away from me.

"Hell, *yes*, disease," I said. "Everybody got passed to everybody else down there. The gods only know what else they were trading."

He spun and faced me. "You need to get tested, too, then."

"I'd already thought of that," I said, although I hadn't. *Oh, gods. I should have stayed. I wonder if the agency has a rape kit?* I rubbed my forehead. *It won't matter. I'm pretty sure Truro's dead.*

*I'm pretty sure I killed them all.*

I sat down on the floor and began weeping again.

"Sage?" Rafe asked uncertainly.

I sucked it up and got back to my feet. "I need a shower," I muttered, pushing past him to the bathroom.

I scrubbed myself until I was raw. That done, I sank to the floor of the shower stall and sobbed until the water ran ice cold.

I remembered a time early in our relationship when I'd been at the end of my rope. I'd gotten so stressed that I threw up all over my last pair of clean jeans. Rafe stayed with me in the bathroom while I finished being sick. Then he helped me run a load of laundry. That was when I fell in love with him.

He didn't come in this time. It was up to me to pick myself up off the shower floor, turn off the water, and wrap myself in a towel.

When I emerged from the bedroom, still in a towel, I saw Rafe out on the balcony. He was fully dressed and talking on his phone.

"Who'd you call?" I asked when he came back in.

"Darrell."

It sounded like another shoe was waiting to drop. "And then who?" I prompted him.

He looked away. "I might have called Shannon."

"Really, Rafe?" *Why don't we just get everybody involved in Sage's humiliation?*

He stood firm against my scorn, his hands-on-hips stance silhouetted by the light from the French doors. "Yes, really, Sage. We've both been through one hell of a traumatic experience, but you...well...you seem to be... Anyway, Darrell and I both think you'd benefit from talking to somebody."

"Patriarchal bullshit from yet another corner," I muttered.

He pointedly ignored me. "You could speak with one of the agency's shrinks, but I thought you might be more comfortable talking to someone you already know."

Of course the agency had counselors on staff. We got into some crazy stuff while deployed – sorry, *working on our projects in the field* – and Darrell the Shaman was not about to let Darrell the Spymaster's troops try to tough it out and keep moving. I remembered hearing a rumor that he'd suffered from PTSD thanks to a deployment in Syria. He might understand better than anyone what we had been through.

Then again, maybe he wouldn't. I would have bet money that no one had ever tried to rape him. Or made him watch while his wife was being sexually abused by another man.

Just thinking about it made me want another shower.

"So is Aunt Shannon coming here?" I asked.

"She can't," he said. "Something about your mother needing her."

"Figures. Of course she'd pick Mom over me." I gripped the edges of towel together at my throat. "I guess I'll have to schedule an appointment with one of the agency's counselors."

"Darrell's already got someone lined up."

I eyed him sidelong. "You guys don't fuck around, do you?"

"Not when someone we love is hurting," he said, meeting my gaze. "Four o'clock this afternoon in Crystal City."

"And you?" I challenged. "When do you see the shrink?"

"My appointment is right after yours."

I swore under my breath. "I guess I'd better get dressed, then, huh?" And I slammed the bedroom door so hard that I knocked a couple of photos off the wall.

Still seething, I yanked clothes out of the closet – slacks and a top, chosen more or less at random since I was too mad to think straight.

I was nearly done dressing when Rafe called my name. "What?" I yelled, only belatedly registering that he sounded kind of upset.

"We got an email from Webb," he said. "There's a video attachment. I don't know whether to show it to you right now or not."

I finished pulling on my socks and went back out to the living room, where Rafe was on his tablet at the breakfast bar. "Let's see it," I said. "This day's already been so shitty that nothing could make it worse."

He looked doubtful. "Do you want to read the email first? Webb says it's not what it looks like. He wants to talk to you about it."

"Just play the fucking thing," I said.

He shrugged and hit play. And that's when I saw my mother acting like a hooker.

"I guess I was wrong," I said. "This day *could* get worse."

"I should have kept my mouth shut," he said.

"Too late now," I told him, more harshly, perhaps, than he deserved. Then I picked up my phone.

"Who are you calling?"

"Darrell," I said. "Fuck the shrink. This is more important. It's past time I had it out with my family, once and for all."

# Chapter 10

The minutes dragged as we waited for Darrell to give us the all-clear. Hilary set up her tablet on the dining room table and teleworked while I made another pot of coffee and drank most of it. Jittery, I roamed the house. No frost crystals clung to our bedroom window today, for which I was absurdly grateful.

My studio beckoned. The application still wasn't done, but I would submit that electronically. I finished packing the model and taped the box shut for mailing as soon as we received the all-clear. Then I opened the app. Then I puttered around, straightening and sorting and putting things away. Then I stared at the app. Then I opened a new project page and threw some stuff together in virtual space to see what stuck. Then I started a load of laundry and did the breakfast dishes, which consisted of our coffee cups, and began wiping down counters that didn't need wiping down.

"Would you please light someplace?" Hilary said, fixing me with an irritated glare.

I froze, one hand on the sponge. "Sorry. I'll go hide in the studio again."

She sighed, stood, and stretched. "It's not you. I can't concentrate, either."

I rinsed the sponge and put it away. "Maybe if we stare at the phone, it will ring."

"Maybe if we watch a movie, it'll ring at the best part."

"Maybe if we go back to bed..."

She crossed the room and put a finger to my lips. Then she stood on her tiptoes and kissed me. "Wow, you're shaking," she said, a moment later.

"Too much coffee," I said.

"That's all it is? I'm hurt." She stuck out her lower lip.

"Oh, baby," I said, my voice low. "It's not the coffee at all. You do things to me..."

She grinned. "That's better," she said, and fiddled with my belt buckle.

"Oh, baby," I said again, and undid her bra with one hand.

Her phone rang at the best part. We ignored it.

A few minutes later – or maybe it was an eternity – my phone rang.

"Seriously, people?" I said, spent. "We're busy here."

Hilary was already rolling off the couch and fishing in my pants for my phone. "It's Darrell," she said, and tossed the phone to me. Then she began getting dressed.

Regretfully, I answered. "Hi, Darrell. Are we free to go?"

"Where the hell were you?" he said in a rush. "I called Hilary's line, but she didn't answer. I thought I told you two to stay put."

"We were busy," I said, emphasizing the last word.

"Oh. *Oh*. Sorry for interrupting."

"We're done now," I said as I grabbed my shorts and maneuvered them on. "Are Sage and Rafe okay?"

"That's why I'm calling," he said. My heart stopped for a moment – until he said, "They're both here with me, and Sage wants to talk to all of you as soon as possible. I've got your parents on the line already. I'm going to put you on holo…"

"Wait!" I said. "Give me thirty seconds." I put the phone down and pulled on the rest of my clothes. Hilary finished buttoning up and combed her fingers through her hair.

As we settled together on the couch again, I could hear Sage saying, voice dripping with disgust, "Only my brother would be having sex at a time like this."

I had a flippant response ready, but I bit it back. I had some idea of what she had just been through; the fact that she could mention sex at all right now spoke volumes about her self-control. Instead, I hit the holo button on my phone, and instantly we appeared to be seated at a big table in some nondescript conference room in the ether. "Hi, everybody," I said. "Sorry to hold you up."

Dad gave me a ghost of his coyote grin. "Hi, guys." He sat on their bed next to Mom, who looked pale and worn out. Aunt Shannon sat in a chair on the other side of Mom. She waved to Hilary and me, and we waved back.

Darrell gave me a solemn wink. I was surprised to see his wife, Tess, sitting next to him, and even more surprised to see Sue and Robbie Duckworth on the other side of Tess. "Wow," I said. "The gang's all here."

Rafe seemed distracted; he kept looking sidelong at my sister, as if gauging how long before she blew, and whether he could get out of range in time to avoid getting hurt. That gave me an insight into their marriage that I wished I didn't have.

"We are now," Darrell said. "Sage, this is your show."

She skipped the preliminaries – or else we had been too late to hear them. In any case, she jumped right in. "Mom," she said, "tell me why I shouldn't be disgusted by the video Webb sent us."

"I said I'd explain," I cut in.

"No," she said. "I want it from the horse's mouth."

"Then you should be asking me," said Dad, and went on to talk about about Jack Rivers, the original Investigator, and how it was really Dad in the scene in the alley, even though it had looked like Mom.

Sage wasn't ready to back down yet. "And what about the first clip?"

"Jack was attempting to rape me," Mom said calmly.

"Which I believe you know something about, now," I cut in, leveling a gaze at Sage.

Her eyes narrowed. "How much did you see?"

"Enough to know you were going to get yourself out of the cabin."

"And what about the day before? Did you see that part, too?" she challenged. "When I actually *was* raped?" Rafe murmured something and put his hands on her shoulders; she shrugged them off.

"No," I said. "I didn't see that part. It must have been horrible."

Her lower lip trembled, which seemed to make her even more angry. "I made that asshole pay," she said, her eyes beginning to show red in their depths. "I made them *all* pay."

"Did anyone survive?" Rafe asked Darrell.

"The women did," Darrell said. "We have them in custody, although we expect to let most of them go. The men did not." He glanced at Sage. "Forensics is determining whether they died from the fire or from their wounds."

"Even Truro Barnstead?" asked Robbie.

Sage rounded on him. "He's the one who raped me! And he was going to do it again. They were *all*..." She covered her face with her hands, and this time when Rafe put an arm around her shoulders, she didn't object.

"Oh, Sage," said Mom, her voice racked with pain. "My poor baby girl." Aunt Shannon looked torn.

Sage scowled at Robbie. "He was *beating* Agnes, Ducky. Why didn't you stop him?"

The Rev. Duckworth's face looked like it wanted to crumple in on itself. "I tried, Sage. I did my best. But by the time I realized how far gone he was, he had taken Agnes and disappeared." He paused for a moment. "I am so sorry he hurt you. I feel like it's my fault. I wish I could do something to help you."

"It's not your fault," Darrell said automatically. "He was one step ahead of us the whole way."

"Who was?" I asked. "Truro Barnstead?"

"No. Whoever's behind all this." He shook his head. "This whole scenario feels familiar, but I can't put my finger on why. It's like they're possessed – Barnstead, Proffitt, Rivers."

"Jack *was* possessed," Aunt Shannon said. "By Tezcatlipoca, years ago. But we convinced Him to let go of Jack, and he seemed much better after that." She looked to Mom and Dad for corroboration.

Mom nodded. "Shannon's right. He even seemed embarrassed that he'd caused us so much trouble. And then he disappeared. We haven't heard a peep out of him in more than thirty years – not 'til Webb ran across him in New Mexico."

"It's not Tezcatlipoca this time," I said. "Not according to Spider Woman, anyway."

Several pairs of eyebrows shot up. "When did you talk to Spider Woman?" Darrell asked.

"In the desert," I said. "On my way to Rivers' camp."

"How did She get there?" he asked. "I thought all access to the gods' world was locked up tight."

"It can't be, can it?" I said reasonably. "Otherwise Iktomi couldn't have left that message for me." The incident on our deck seemed like a lifetime ago. "Anyway, Spider Woman said Loki can't watch all the exits all the time."

Tess gripped Darrell's arm. "If They can find a way out, we could find a way in."

"I hope so. I miss Gaia," Sue said.

Heads nodded around the table. Tess snorted. "I never thought I'd miss Morrigan, but I do."

Mom seemed to pull in on herself. I imagined she missed White Buffalo Calf Pipe Woman, but for different reasons.

I let the silence linger for a moment. Then I said, "There may be a portal near Mesa Verde."

Dad looked stunned for a moment. "Of course! The *sipapu*," he said. "I should have thought of that." A *sipapu*, I knew, was a hole in the floor of many kivas built by the Anasazi, who were ancestors to the present-day Hopi. Its practical use was for ventilation, but in spiritual terms, it symbolized the first *sipapu* through which the Anasazi, or *their* ancestors, entered our world from the previous level of creation. The gods may have eventually repurposed the original *sipapu* as a portal to Their own world – either in ancient times, or after the portal near Boulder was sealed.

"Has Rivers' body been found?" I asked Darrell.

"No," he said. "And I wanted to ask you about that. When you last saw Rivers, where was he?"

I looked at Dad. "He was inside the pole barn, in a wire mesh cage. The sort of thing you'd use as a kennel for a large dog."

"And you didn't let him out."

"There wasn't time. Proffitt's minions were barreling toward us so fast that we concentrated on getting airborne. The flood washed our pursuers away first, but the pole barn went immediately afterward. There wasn't time to go back," I repeated.

"And when you last saw the cage, it was locked," said Darrell.

"Yeah. Why?"

Darrell sat back. "Because the cage showed up way downstream from the other wreckage. It was battered but intact, and the door was still locked. But Rivers wasn't inside."

"It's like he went poof and disappeared," said Tess, her fingers springing open on the word *poof*.

"Disappeared," I said slowly as I made the connections, "or dissipated. Like smoke."

"What are you thinking?" Dad asked.

I looked around the virtual conference room. I think it was seeing all these people together again – Darrell and Tess, Sue and Robbie, and my family – that brought the memory to the fore. "Remember the time we visited Washington? When Mom was advising Tess on her testimony before Congress?"

Tess smiled. "You made me a bracelet. I still have it."

"Good," I said. That bracelet was a pocket universe which contained an entrance to the web of creation. "Keep it safe, in case something happens to me."

"Webb?" Hilary asked, her eyes wide and her hand on my shoulder.

"There's nothing to worry about, Hotaru," I told her. "It's insurance, that's all." I took her hand in mine as I turned back to the group. "There was an entity causing all the trouble, remember? I made a special net for it – one that could hold a being made of smoke."

"Lucifer," Tess said. This Lucifer wasn't a devil in the old Christian sense. He was an entity who wanted to be a god so badly that he went about gathering followers by any means necessary. His specialties were fear and hatred, ginned up in the usual way: by setting human beings against one another, over superficial differences like skin color and religious affiliation. I had been taught that evil was a religious construct, but Lucifer was the closest to an evil being I've ever met. Now that I thought about it, I realized this Neo-Atheist thing was right up his alley.

"We turned him over to the gods," Tess continued. "They were supposed to lock him up."

I nodded. "Spider Woman told me She wasn't sure I had the strength to defeat the Neo-Atheists – partly because of their protector, who She said was no longer under the gods' control."

"Who let him out?" Dad asked, brow furrowed.

"Who was in charge of keeping track of him?" I asked at the same time.

"Loki," chorused Darrell, Tess, Sue and Robbie.

I groaned. "That explains everything," I said. "He could have set Lucifer free to distract us while He sets Ragnarok in motion."

Darrell glanced at the tablet in front of him. "There's a new video," he said. "I'll patch it in so we can watch it together."

"Splendid," my sister muttered. Then the conference room vanished, replaced by a virtual screen.

A woman's face filled it. It was lit from below, like when you hold a flashlight under your chin before you tell a ghost story. I didn't recognize her, but I heard Sage say, "That's Emmy!"

Beside me, Hilary nodded. "Emmy Proffitt. Ward's wife – or widow, now, I guess. She was in our class, too." Then we all went quiet to hear what she had to say.

"This message is directed at you, Sage Orloff," the woman said, her voice venomous, "and to all those working with you. You may have killed my husband, but you haven't killed the things he stood for. Those things live on in me. Our movement is growing like wildfire, with more units being formed every day, all over the world."

"Bullshit," Darrell interjected.

"Soon," Emmy went on, "the global Neo-Atheist Movement will rule the Earth, and make it into the kind of place it used to be – back when morality meant something."

Sage and Rafe both snorted.

"And on that day, you'll think my husband has come back from the dead!" said Emmy.

Another face filled the screen. "As I have," said Jack Rivers. I heard my mother suck in a breath. "I'm coming for you, Naomi. You and your family – your precious Joseph, your daughter Sage and her Raven husband, and your son Webb, his girlfriend, and the child she carries – they are all in my crosshairs. And there will be no escape. Not this time."

The screen split, with Emmy's face on one side and Rivers' face on the other. "Because we are everywhere, all the time," they intoned together. "Everywhere, all the time. Everywhere, all the time." The screen went dark. Then, as a cock crowed, the Neo-Atheists' logo faded in and faded out again.

The conference room view came back, revealing varying expressions of horror and dismay – but only Aunt Shannon appeared to want to bolt. "Shannon, what is it?" Darrell asked.

"That's the third cock crow," she said.

"Tell us what that means."

"It's…" She swallowed and composed herself, and then started again. "In the old tales, Ragnarok begins this way: First, there will be winter with no summer for three years straight. Then society will break down – even family members will fight one another." I glanced between Mom and Sage; they wore identical expressions of dismay. "A wolf will devour the sun and his brother will eat the moon. Those are the harbingers."

"We've escaped the endless winter," Sue said, nodding to Sage, Rafe, Hilary and me, "thanks to you all. And the sun and moon are still up in the sky."

"Here, yes," Aunt Shannon said. "But we don't know what's happening in the gods' world. Anyway, next, the parties are notified that it's on. One cock will crow to notify the Giants; a second will crow to notify the gods; and the third will crow to raise the dead."

Emmy's and Rivers' comments about coming back from the dead now resonated in a different way for me.

"And then what?" asked Sue.

"Earthquakes," said Aunt Shannon, "as the Midgard Serpent finds its way to the battle. That releases the wolf Fenrir, who is Loki's son. They all converge on the battlefield, where Heimdall blows his horn and the war begins."

"And the world ends," said Robbie. "Everybody dies, including humanity."

"Except for a few gods who reboot the Earth," said Aunt Shannon. "But the three cock crows mean it's on."

"We need to get into the gods' world," said Tess.

"It might already be too late," Aunt Shannon said.

"We need to stop Lucifer first," Robbie said. "And let's not put Loki in charge of keeping an eye on him this time."

"You can leave that to me," I said.

Hilary rounded on me. "Are you crazy?"

"Probably," I said, squeezing her hand again. "But not about this. Look." I turned to the group, acutely aware that mine was the youngest face here. "I know some of you think I'm still a kid. The hair probably doesn't help." I ruffled my fingers across my mop of curls. Hilary's fingers brushed mine aside and tenderly smoothed my hair back; I kissed the top of her head before resuming. "But just like Sage, I've been at this all my life. Tess, I was six years old when I made that bracelet for you."

"I remember," she said.

"And now I'm thirty-five," I said quickly, before she could reminisce about how adorable I'd been back then. "When I was a kid, I operated on instinct. I didn't know how I knew to make the things I did, or how I got them to work the way they did. And I sure didn't know how I knew the future. But I've been asking a lot of questions since then." I turned to Mom and Dad. "Those summers I spent with Grandpa Drew and Leonard when I was in middle school? I know you guys sent me up to Pine Ridge to soak up Lakota culture – and I did – but I also spent quite a bit of time learning about my powers. Leonard taught me a lot." I made a mental note to thank him formally for the help – assuming I survived.

"You guys all do amazing things every day, as a matter of course," I went on, "whereas I've been the family joke. 'Oh, look at little Webb. Knitting is his superpower – isn't that cute?'" I put on a squeaky voice, and dropped it just as fast. "And that's fine. It's been fun being the class clown. There's a place for laughter, after all, even when things are bleakest. So the cover has served my purposes well.

"Until now." I leaned in. "Now, Lucifer thinks I'm a pushover. So first, he found a way into my dreams. That's not all that hard to do, actually – most people don't know how to put up a psychic barrier, let alone keep it activated while they sleep. I know how, but I've gotten sloppy about it because things have been so quiet over the past few years. But Loki exploited my carelessness, and Lucifer followed Him in." I shook my head ruefully.

"But then Lucifer did something He shouldn't have been able to do." I paused, my lips quirking up on one side. "I'm giving away one of my trade secrets here, I hope you know." Then I got serious again. "One of the ways I read the future is to copy the relevant strands of the web of the Universe and put the copies into a sort of timestream. It's a simulation of the real thing, so if I happen to pull a strand here or there, it doesn't affect reality. But it does let me see how the individual streams interact, and I can tell how events might fall out differently if one or more factors change. With me so far?" I looked around the table. A number of pairs of eyes had widened, but no one looked lost. Satisfied, I proceeded. "Good. Early Monday morning, I entered my simulation and started poking around. Before I knew what was happening, something threw me into Sage's timeline and let me see part of her trial. Then it kicked me out again. It was the being I've been calling the smoke monster – the one we now know is Lucifer. He spoke to me. Threatened me." *I am stronger than you know. Soon…we will meet again soon…and then you will know me, and I will laugh as you pray to your puny gods to save you!*

I took a deep breath and resumed. "As I said, he shouldn't have been able to do that. The simulations aren't real; they don't exist anywhere but in my own mind." I heard Hilary suck in a breath as she grasped the implications of that – Lucifer having been inside my head and all – but I plowed on. "I've been trying to figure out how he got in, but now I think I know." I nodded at Tess again. "And your bracelet was the key. What you see when you wear it is also a simulation of the Universal web, albeit in a different format. And it's live – just as the one in my head is live. It's connected to the real web – so that if things change in real life, they'll show up immediately in the simulation. When I was six, I didn't know how to make one any other way." I curled my lip again. "But I do now. And if this works, I can guarantee Lucifer won't trouble anyone ever again."

Darrell rubbed the back of his neck. "Well," he said, "about eighty-five percent of that went over my head, but…"

"No," Tess said in wonder. "It makes sense to me."

I smiled gratefully at her. She was the only person in the room with whom I'd ever shared any of this, and she hadn't known the mechanics behind it – all she knew was that her bracelet showed her the future.

"Should we trust him with this?" Darrell asked her.

"Oh, yeah," she said. "Abso-fucking-lutely. He's the real deal, sweetheart. If he says he can mousetrap Lucifer, I believe him."

"And I know better than to argue with you."

"You'd damn well better by now."

They shared a grin, and then Darrell turned to me. "It's all yours, Webb, with our thanks. Is there anything we can do to help?"

"I could use some help brainstorming a way to lure him in," I said. "And somebody please get a picture of Sage for me." For my sister was staring at me in open-mouthed wonder.

Rafe waggled his eyebrows. "Hold that pose, honey," he said, as he pulled out his phone to do the honors.

She flinched at the flash and rolled her eyes at us. Then she regarded me again. "Still waters run deep, huh, little brother?"

I bowed from the waist. "Thank you! I'll be here all week."

"Before we move on," Mom put in, "I'd like a word with my children."

"Oh, fuck," said Sage, and sat back with her arms crossed.

Darrell shrugged. "We can take a break. Five minutes okay, Naomi? Ten?"

"I hope it won't take ten," she said, eyeing my sister.

"Everybody back here in ten minutes," Darrell said, and pushed a button we couldn't see. Then he and Tess got up and left the room, closing the door behind them. Now it was just Sage and Rafe; Mom, Dad, and Aunt Shannon; and Hilary and me.

"I'll make tea," Aunt Shannon said, starting up out of her chair.

Mom put a hand on her arm. "No, Shannon. Please stay." Aunt Shannon reluctantly sat back down.

"Maybe she needs the restroom, Mom," I said, trying to lighten the mood.

"I'm fine," Aunt Shannon said.

"Don't change the subject," Mom said.

I raised my hands in surrender. "Okay. Sorry. Go, Mom. It's your show."

She looked at Dad, who had adopted his inscrutable Indian expression. Rafe looked like a man who had been through hell on no sleep – which was an apt description of his situation, come to think of it. Beside me, Hilary seemed to have shrunken into the couch cushions.

Sage still had her arms crossed and was regarding Mom from under her eyelashes.

"Don't sulk, Sage," Mom said.

"Don't tell me what to do, Mom," Sage returned.

I was done with both of them. "Look, can we all act like adults?" I said. "Mom's got some tough news for you, big sister. Sit up and take it like the grownup you claim you are."

Eyes wide, Sage sat up and saluted. "Yes sir, little brother, sir," she said.

I waited, motionless, until she dropped the salute. "Go, Mom," I said again.

Mom looked down at her fingernails. "I've got cancer."

Sage eyed her. "How bad?" she asked, her tone less combative than a minute before.

"Bad," said Mom. "We've done everything we can, and we're still doing everything we can, but..." She raised her hands in a helpless gesture.

"You're...?" Sage stopped.

"Dying," I finished for her. Apparently I was the only one who could say it.

"Oh, Mom," she said faintly. And then her anger blazed up again. "Where the hell is the goddess? Why isn't She doing something about it?"

Dad shook his head. "The gods are gone, Sage."

"But they've only been gone for a couple of weeks! How long have you been sick?"

"It's an aggressive cancer," Aunt Shannon put in. "I've never seen anything like it."

"Can't *you* cure her?" Sage asked.

"I've tried," Aunt Shannon said, "but it just keeps roaring back."

"I think I know why," I said, before my sister could ream Aunt Shannon. All eyes turned to me. "I think Someone is controlling the disease."

"You've seen this?" Dad said, eyebrows raised.

"I've seen evidence, yes," I said evenly. "Then Lucifer yanked me into Sage's timeline, and things have been a little crazy since then. Otherwise I would have called you right away."

"Is it Lucifer who's interfering?" Aunt Shannon asked.

I shook my head. "I didn't recognize the signature. It's not a goddess I've had any dealings with before."

"Goddess?" Mom asked. At my nod, she snorted softly. "Well, that narrows it down. You'll keep an eye out for me, won't you?"

"Of course, Mom," I said.

"Good. I knew I could count on you." She smiled at me gratefully, and then turned to Sage. "I need your help, too."

My sister began shaking her head. "If this is about that thing we discussed before…"

"But…"

"No!" Sage said. "I'm not going to have a baby on command, just because White Buffalo Calf Pipe Woman wants another heir! And I can't believe you would do this to me now."

"What am I doing to you?" Mom asked.

"You're trying to guilt me into cooperating because you're sick!"

I knew that was what Sage was driving at, even before she said it. I didn't think that was Mom's intent – not consciously, at least – but I could see how Sage could think it was.

Unfortunately, Mom's next words did nothing to dispel my sister's suspicion. "Honey, it's just that time is growing short. And I need all the leverage I can get with the gods if I'm going to avert Ragnarok!"

"How much time?" I asked.

Heads turned toward me. It was Aunt Shannon who answered. "Weeks. Maybe a month."

That was definitely not what I'd seen in the timeline. But my simulation was no guarantee.

Hilary had placed one hand on her belly; I covered it with one of mine. We exchanged a look of dismay. "I won't accept that," I said, turning to my parents. "My mother will not die before she's met her grandchild, if I have anything to say about it."

"Good for you," Sage said. "I'm out." She got up and headed for the door. "I'll send Darrell back in."

"Sage!" Mom called.

My sister turned back to face her. She was clutching the doorjamb with one hand and her middle with the other, and tears were running down her cheeks. The sight of Sage crying shocked me; I couldn't remember the last time I'd seen her cry. "Look," she said shakily, "I've had a really tough day, and I'm not at my best right now. Rafe and I are…" She hunched her shoulders, as if that would complete the sentence. The man in question stared at his hands. "And all the stuff this morning, and we just got back, and now you." She sucked in a breath. "I can't help you right now, Mom," she said. "I need to take care of myself first. I'm supposed to see a counselor in, like, an hour. Maybe…" She shut her eyes. "No. I won't promise anything. At least you've got Webb. He seems capable enough." Her voice broke on the word *capable*, and she turned again to go.

"I love you, Sage," Mom said. She was crying, too. "I wish I were there with you."

"I love you, too, Mom," Sage said, without turning back. Then she was gone.

In the ensuing silence, Aunt Shannon handed out tissues to Mom and Dad. Rafe looked up and said, "It hasn't been good between us for a while, actually."

"Not a good time to bring a baby into it," Aunt Shannon said.

"No," said Rafe. "Thanks for understanding."

"Do you need to go after her?" Dad asked.

"Honestly? I think she's better off just seeing the counselor."

"What about you?" Aunt Shannon said. "Are *you* seeing a counselor?"

He nodded and looked down at his hands again. "For the past few months, yeah."

After a few moments, I said, "Well, you've gotta hand it to my sister. She sure knows how to suck the energy out of a room." In the nervous laughter that followed, I said to Rafe, "Are you in? The Loki and Lucifer thing, I mean."

His smile faded, and he regarded me fiercely. "You bet I am. I want those sick bastards to suffer for what they did to my wife."

"So do I," I said, as Tess and Darrell came in. "So do I."

# Chapter 11

Late that night, I settled myself on the couch. "Want to sit here with me?" I asked Hilary. I patted the spot next to me in invitation.

"Will it help?"

"Actually," I said, "you'll probably distract me. You know how distracting you are, baby."

"Cool it, tiger," she said, dropping a kiss on my forehead. "I'll wait for you in bed."

"Oh, like that will help me keep my mind on business," I called as she made her way down the hallway.

"Who said I wanted to?" she said in a sultry voice.

I grinned and shifted, getting into a more comfortable position. I had just closed my eyes when Hilary said at my elbow, "Honey?"

"Yeah, baby?"

"Should I come and wake you in an hour or something?"

I opened my eyes. "You're really worried, aren't you?"

She changed her balance from one foot to the other. "Yeah."

"But it's never bothered you before." I swept one hand toward my usual setup: a cup of coffee and a candle on the coffee table. The candle served as a focal point if I was having trouble calming my thoughts. Plus it added that certain *je ne sais pas*. The coffee was for…well, I drink a lot of coffee.

She looked away. "I never knew what you were doing before."

She had a point. Early in our relationship, she had asked about my little ritual, and I had told her I was meditating – which was true, as far as it went. Which wasn't very far. "Come and sit," I said, and this time she did. "I love you," I said, "and you know I've done this thousands of times. You've seen me do it. And I've always come back to you, haven't I?"

"Yeah, but…"

"And you know I would tell you if I was going to do something really dangerous, right?"

She snorted. "Not a chance."

"See? You know me so well, it's scary."

She smacked me on the chest, then picked up my arm and put it around her. "Can you do it if I stay right here?"

"You want to stay?" This was new. "It's not like you can come in after me if something goes wrong, y'know."

"I know," she said, nestling against me.

I reflected on how it probably would be good to have an anchor in the real world, at least this once. "Okay," I said. Then I closed my eyes again.

Even with Hilary next to me, I slipped into the timestream with no trouble at all. And as I had hoped, my buddy, the little glowing spider, was there to greet me. "Is he here?" I asked.

Chittering, the spider bobbed up and down. I took that as a yes.

After Sage left, our meeting hadn't lasted very long. Darrell and Rafe promised to put the word out that JAF-H/D was on the lookout for both Jack Rivers and Emmy Proffitt, and that the agency had hired a special investigator who was adept at tracing timestreams. Tess had dutifully made sure the story ran on her network several times, despite the fact that her producers and anchors complained about the lack of detail. She wasn't happy about using them as bait, but she'd extracted a promise from Darrell that NWNN would have dibs on the whole story as soon as I was done – one way or the other.

"And are we ready to close the back door?" I asked my little buddy.

In reply, he extended a glowing line well above the slightly duller timelines. I grabbed it, and he pulled me along behind him upstream, if you will, to the place where my simulation drew from the real web.

It wasn't a door or a portal so much as a well, although that's not a good description, either. My simulation slopes at one end to a sort of hole or tube. If you could pass through the hole – which you can't, both because it's not real and because it would be impossible to fight against the current – you would land on the Universal web. You could ride the current into my simulation, assuming you could find the door or portal or bottom of the well, and assuming you could stand the force of the time current. I had originally assumed nothing would be able to survive, but then I'd never thought I'd need protection against a smoke being.

Anyway, it was time to shut it down. I reached into a pocket of my cargo pants and brought out a pair of scissors. Then I nodded to my buddy, who spun out a gossamer line. I took the end and braced myself as he played out more line, and began wrapping it around the timestreams gushing forth from the well. Once he had anchored my end solidly against unwinding, I pulled strong cord from a different pocket and rapidly worked it up into a cover to fit the diameter of the opening of the portal.

At last, the little spider cut his line and swung back to me. He picked up one end of my portal cover; I picked up my scissors and sliced through the timestream on the side nearest the portal. The bound end dropped, the loose ends fell back through the portal, and the spider and I slapped the cover across the opening. A stitch here and there, and the cover blended seamlessly with the walls of the simulation. I realized I'd been holding my breath, and let it go in an explosive sigh of relief. The spider held up one leg, and I gently high-fived him. Then I pocketed my scissors and let him tow me back to where I'd come in.

Lucifer was waiting for me. "So," said His Smokiness in a menacing voice, "we meet at last, little spider. Do you know me now?"

"Oh, yeah," I said casually. "Hi, Lucifer. How've you been?"

This was clearly not the reaction he expected, but he recovered swiftly. "You think to distract me with your banter," he said, "but it won't work. I have invaded your mind and mastered your domain. Think on that, and be dismayed!" Amid raucous laughter, he picked me up with nonexistent hands and threw me high in the air. "You wanted to find our mutual friend Jack Rivers?" he taunted. "Here he is!" And my support was gone. I plummeted what felt like several stories, landing in a part of the timestream I didn't recognize. This was not a stream I had captured, and for a moment I was frightened. Lucifer must have threaded a few more streams into my simulation. Maybe a lot more.

Then I relaxed. He might have figured out the mechanism, but he didn't know how the system worked. I was sure he didn't realize that by pulling a timestream in here, he was only making a copy. He didn't know that anything he changed in here had no bearing at all on events in the real world.

And so it was with equanimity that I plunged into a dark stream and found myself in a cave – no, a kiva – with Jack Rivers.

Rivers took no notice of me; I was as insubstantial now as I had been when viewing Sage's ordeal. I took a seat on the floor and studied him. While the years had been kind to my parents – at least up until the last few years for Mom – Rivers had clearly had a tougher go of it. He might have been of medium height, had he stood up straight, but his shoulders were rounded so that he walked in a stoop. His hair and beard were white, his eyes a faded brown. He wore the same flannel shirt and jeans I'd seen him in when he was caged in the pole barn, and the flood had not improved their condition.

He sat before a meager fire, his head bowed. It took me a minute to realize he was chained, hand and foot. I guess his captors hadn't had time to buy another dog crate yet.

Light appeared at an entrance to the chamber – a propane lantern, judging by the hissing sound – and Rivers sprang to his feet. "Joseph?" he crooned, his voice cunning. "Come on in. I've got a surprise for you and Naomi."

"Shut up, old man," a man growled from around the corner. "Here's your dinner." And someone slid a tin plate full of stew into the room. At least, I assumed it was stew; it was brown, and some of it sloshed over the edge when the plate came to a stop.

Rivers picked up the plate and poured the food into his mouth, dribbling down his chin. They hadn't given him a spoon. He wiped his mouth on his tattered shirt sleeve and called out, "I need to make another video. I have more to say to Naomi. More to say to Joseph." No response. "Do you have my DVDs? I can't find them."

"Shut up, old man," the man around the corner growled again. "I told you, everything washed away in the flood."

"But I need my DVDs," Rivers whined. "They're my insurance."

"Jesus," the man muttered. "I told you a hundred times, we don't need your piece of shit DVDs. Boss has got everything in his brain. We can just tap into it any time we want."

Another man spoke – younger, less gruff. "Why do we keep this crazy old loon around, anyway, Murray?"

"I told you a hundred times, McClung. Boss says we need him, so we keep him." He raised his voice. "Hey, old man. You done eating? Toss your plate back out here."

Rivers had been licking the plate. Now he stood. Gripping the rim with his chained hands, he planted his feet, turned the upper half of his body, and flung the plate out the doorway. It made quite a racket as it ricocheted off the corridor's walls, making the men yell, until it finally spun to a stop.

"I told you a hundred times not to do that, old man!" Murray yelled. "You're gonna miss breakfast again, until you learn!" He and McClung moved off, taking the lantern with them. "And that's why you don't let him see you," Murray told McClung. "For a crazy old coot, he's got one hell of an aim."

"Want to make a video," Rivers muttered as he sat back down before his fire. "Want to see Naomi."

I had no time to reflect on what I'd seen before I was yanked out of Rivers' timestream and thrown high in the air. Lucifer surrounded me with his smoke, and laughed when I coughed. "See? I'm your friend, little spider," he said. "See how helpful I can be? Why, I'll even let you see the other person you're looking for!" And down I went again, this time into a hotel room where half a dozen women in nightgowns gazed at a television monitor set to NWNN. On the screen was a reporter somewhere in South Carolina, giving the official version of the events that had transpired there that morning. I assumed these were the widows of the Neo-Atheists who had died in the raid. Sage, I was sure, would know them all, but the only one I recognized was Emmy Proffitt.

"That's not what happened," she said now, pointing at the screen. "Gemma killed our husbands. Right?"

"All I saw was a giant bird setting the cabin afire," one of the women said.

"Yes," Emmy said impatiently. "That was Gemma. Her real name is Sage Orloff and she owns that giant bird." Which was not entirely untrue, I thought. "Didn't you see them flying away together? Like a witch and her familiar."

"We don't believe in witches, Emmy," the woman said again.

"We don't believe in *gods*, Tansy," Emmy said. "Witches aren't *gods*."

"We don't believe in witches, either," another of the women said. "The news is all lies, anyway. Why are we watching this?" She yawned. "I'm turning in."

"Agnes Barnstead," Emmy cried. "How can you be so dismissive when we've all just lost our husbands? We need to stick together! We need to take our revenge on Ted and Gemma. Don't you miss Truro?"

That name rang a bell. I looked more closely at Agnes and saw the unmistakable mottling of healing bruises on her face. "No," she said shortly. "No, I don't, Emmy. He beat me any chance he got, and stuck his dick into anything that wore a skirt. Including all of you." She sought to make eye contact with each woman in turn, but all of them except Emmy turned away. One woman began to cry softly. "I can't tell you how glad I am to be rid of Truro Barnstead. I'm changing back to my maiden name as soon as I get home. Goodnight." She looked at the weeping woman. "Coming, Tina?"

Tina nodded and followed Agnes out into the hallway. A moment later, the woman named Tansy stalked off after them.

As soon as the door shut behind her, Emmy turned to the two remaining women and said, "Tomorrow, they're dead. The Boss is going to help us."

I wasn't surprised this time when I shot up out of the timestream. And this vignette confirmed my suspicions nicely: Not only was Murray and McClung's boss the same entity that had promised to help Emmy Proffitt kill the widows who opposed her, but I also knew who was feeding the Neo-Atheists video of my parents at impossible angles.

So I felt no compunction at all to be pleasant to Lucifer when he pulled me once again into his smoky embrace. "Seen enough, little spider?" he asked gleefully.

"I have indeed," I said, as a gossamer thread penetrated his cloud above my head. "And I have some news for you."

"Oh?" he said in a bored tone. "What's that?"

I grasped my lifeline and said, "You're not going anywhere."

Lucifer roared as I exited my simulation for the last time, sealing the entrance behind me as if it had never existed. Then I squeezed it on all sides, packing it smaller and smaller until it was an infinitesimal dot. With one final squeeze, it winked out.

My spider pal landed on my sleeve. I high-fived him again. "Thanks, buddy," I said. He waved, and then pulled me back to *now*.

Exhausted, I opened my eyes. Hilary was still beside me, asleep, with her head against my shoulder. The candle had burned unevenly; it had melted through low on one side and dumped a river of wax as it guttered out. The wax had spread across the top of the coffee table and puddled around the base of my mug.

I pulled the mug free and downed the cold coffee; caffeine is caffeine, after all, and it would serve to stave off the massive headache I sometimes had after one of these sessions. I suspected this one, if left untreated, would be a doozy.

"Hey," I said softly as I placed the mug back in its ring of wax. "Hotaru."

Her head came up. "You're back," she said, and smiled. "I'm so glad."

"Me, too," I said, and kissed her temple. "Let's go to bed."

For the first time in days, neither dreams nor portents troubled my sleep.

# Chapter 12

The following day was Wednesday, the day my grant application was due.

Before Hilary even got out of bed, I tossed some cucumbers out the back door for Enkou and called Darrell. Once he heard my report, he gave us the all-clear to resume our daily activities. He also promised to notify the local authorities about Emmy Proffitt and her crew, and assured me the women who had stood up to her would be free to go. And he said he would relay the information to Sage and Rafe. He thought Sage would be glad to hear the fates of the Neo-Atheists' wives. I wasn't so sure about that.

As for Jack Rivers, Darrell and I agreed his whereabouts were a puzzle best left for another day. Although it would have to be soon; now that Lucifer was neutralized, our next priority was finding a portal into the gods' realm.

*Our* next priority? I was starting to sound like one of the members of Mom's famous woo-woo team. I told myself to watch it, or else the real heroes in this outfit would start taking me seriously.

I called my parents myself – and that's when my day went off the rails.

"Webb!" Mom said. "Thank the gods. I was about to call you. I need you to do something for me today."

"What?" I said suspiciously.

"I need you to drive me to the Holts' this morning," she said.

"Aw, Mom, come on," I said, knowing I was whining. "My grant application is due today! I cannot miss this deadline! Can't Aunt Shannon take you instead?"

"Shannon is out on a midwife call," Mom said, a touch of asperity in her voice. "She left late last night, and who knows how long that baby will take to get here?"

"What about Uncle George?"

"George and your father are both *working*," she said.

"They ought to retire," I grumbled. "Then *they* could be at your beck and call, instead of me."

Mom chose to ignore that. "The reception starts at noon," she said, "so I'll need you here by eleven."

It occurred to me that I had an honest-to-gods out. "I can't do it, Mom, seriously," I said. "I don't have a car." Sometime over the past couple of days, we'd heard from the mechanic in Farmington who'd taken custody of the carcass of my hovercar. He'd pronounced poor old Fossil dead on arrival, and of course my insurance company had yet to pay. Not that we'd have had time to go car-shopping, anyway.

Mom paused for a split second. Then she covered the mouthpiece and yelled, "Joseph!" A few moments later, she was back on the line. "Your father is going to pick you up. You can drop him off at work, then circle back here."

"Where's he working this week?" I asked.

"Longmont."

I looked at the clock and did the math. It was doable, but just barely. "All right," I said, resigned. "If he's here by nine, I can take you."

"He'll be there by 8:30," Mom promised. "Thank you, Webb. I don't know what I'd do if I didn't have you to rely on." Then she ended the call.

I put down the phone as Hilary breezed into the kitchen. "Why the long face?" she asked, getting herself some cereal.

"Mom wants me to squire her to some reception at the Holts' place." I took a seat at the dinette set, propped an elbow on the edge of the table, and sunk my chin into my hand.

"You're not planning to take my car, are you? I have some errands to run."

"No, of course not. Dad's driving up here so I can take *him* to work, drive back to Golden to pick up Mom, and then drive her into Denver."

"Sounds unnecessarily convoluted," she offered.

"It's ridiculous. Mom needs to figure out another way to do this."

"Maybe it's time for them to think about giving up the place in Golden and moving closer to town."

I shook my head – a neat trick when your chin is virtually immobilized. "They'll never do it. Dad needs the room to run." I sprawled back in my chair. "Anyway, this is going to make filing the grant application dicier than I expected. The model's boxed up and ready to go in the mail, but I have to submit the app electronically by five o'clock."

"I can mail the model," Hilary said. "The post office is right on my way."

"Would you? That would make my life so much easier."

"Of course," she said, a little surprised. "Why wouldn't I? We're a team, Webb."

"Of course we are," I said automatically.

Dad arrived as Hilary was leaving. He had half a cup of coffee, and then we were off.

The building site, as it turned out, was east of Longmont. But I still thought I could make it to Golden in time. I dropped Dad off and set his hovercar to cruising altitude, and made it to the homestead with ten minutes to spare.

"Good! You're here," said Mom, meeting me at the door. "I'm so grateful that I can depend on you." She was all decked out in her best suit, which hung a little slack on her these days. Mom had never been a clotheshorse, but she knew how to dress up when circumstances dictated it.

Now she eyed my cargo pants and down vest. "You're not going in *that*, are you?"

I raised my hands to ward her off. "Hey, I'm just the driver."

"You are not. You're my escort, Webb. You can't walk in there looking like a derelict." She gave me a gentle push toward the stairs. "Go find a jacket and tie, at least. Something."

I scowled, even as I began to mount the stairs. "Who's this reception for, anyway?"

"Some mucky-muck from Iceland. I'll find the invitation while you're dressing."

As soon as she said *Iceland*, I stopped and stared at Mom, while flashing on my nightmare of the hatchet-faced people and their leader, who had tried to eat me up.

"Go on!" she urged.

At least I'd gotten one good night's sleep before the crazy stuff started again.

I knew I had a pair of black cargo pants in the back of my old closet, which was good; I wasn't about to go to this thing unarmed. Rapidly, I transferred all my bits and bobs from one pair of pants to the other, and put them on. Further closet excavations turned up the shirt, tie, and dress shoes I'd worn for Sage's wedding, and a maroon sport coat that more or less went with the tie. I brushed at my hair and gave up.

"This is as good as it gets," I told Mom as I descended the staircase.

"It's fine," she said. "And I apologize. I should have been more explicit in my instructions. Let's go."

That first panhandler we had seen the week before had apparently given other people ideas. We passed no fewer than eight on our way to the Holts' residence.

Mom clucked her tongue after the third one. Then she said, "How did it go with Lucifer?"

I'd filled in Dad on the drive to Longmont, but of course Mom hadn't been with us. So I gave her the highlights, including the news that Jack Rivers had survived the flood.

"We need to take care of Jack," she said quietly, as I turned onto the street where the Holts lived. I couldn't tell by her tone whether she meant to neutralize him or adopt him.

"Darrell's on it," I said.

"Good."

The Secret Service agents let us in the gate, and a valet – hired for the occasion, I supposed – relieved me of the car keys and made off with Dad's vehicle. I would rather have parked the thing myself, but another car pulled up behind us and got the same treatment. If it was a trap, I concluded, we were all trapped. Which was not a comforting thought.

We were directed up the grand staircase to a large, open room. Across from the entrance was a wall of windows, the heavy drapes parted to reveal a view of the snowcapped Rockies. One thing we didn't get in Golden, because we were in the foothills, was this sort of vista – although we had a sweeping view of the lights of Denver, stunning in its own way, that you couldn't get from downtown.

A buffet was set up at one end of the room, a drinks station was set up at the other, and between us and the food was the inevitable receiving line. At the head of the line stood the President and his number-one son. Both were about my height, so they were easy to spot. I could tell Antonia stood between them because I caught a glimpse of her dark hair now and again. The one person I couldn't see was the guest of honor; he or she was on the other side of the President, and short enough that he completely blocked the guest from view.

"Hey, Ms. Curtis! Hey, Webb!" Roman grabbed our hands and shook them, a grin splitting his face. "Glad to see you here. These things are always kind of stuffy. I appreciate seeing a familiar face."

"Good to see you, too, Roman," I said, noting the down vest and jeans he wore. His mother hadn't made *him* change clothes. I indicated the guitar strapped to his back. "So you're the entertainment?"

"Can you believe it?" he said. "Mom told me they hadn't hired a band for this thing. And I said, 'Who has a reception without a band?' So I volunteered to be the band."

"She said okay?" Mom said, surprised.

Roman leaned in toward her ear, one hand beside his mouth. "I didn't give her a chance to say no," he said in a confidential tone.

They exchanged smiles as Roman pulled his guitar around. "Gotta go be the strolling musician now. Nice to see you both. We'll talk later." His last comment appeared to be aimed at me. He strummed a chord, nodded to us, and struck up a tune as he wandered off.

"Antonia has her hands full with that one," Mom said with a sigh. Then she patted my arm. "Thank the gods you're nothing like him."

I frowned at her. That was the third time in five hours that she had alluded to my presumed dependability. "What have you got up your sleeve, anyway?" I asked.

"Rex! Hi," she said, reaching past me to shake the hand of the heir apparent. I hadn't realized it, but we'd reached the head of the line as we chatted with Roman.

"Hello, Ms. Curtis," he intoned in his faux baritone. "Hello, Webb. How are things? Still in Boulder?"

I shook his hand and smiled sadly. "I am, Rex, sorry. I still can't vote for you."

"Pity. Well, you may have that chance before long, even if you don't move to Denver."

"Oh?" Mom said. "The rumors are true, then? You're planning a run for the U.S. Senate?"

He inclined his head modestly. "It's far too early for a formal announcement. But yes, I'm testing the waters, looking for endorsements and financial support from certain key people."

"Oh, don't be tiresome, Rex," Antonia cut in, rescuing Mom from having to declare that she preferred her politicians to have brains, thanks very much. She and Mom then squeed like teenagers and hugged as if they hadn't seen each other in years. Cameras flashed around us to capture the joyous moment.

Then it was my turn for a hug from Antonia. "You look dapper," she told me as she straightened my lapels. "I tried to get Roman to change, but…"

"Roman will never change," I said, finishing her sentence for her.

"There you have it," she said. "Nice to see you." And it was on to the President, who clapped me on the shoulder and welcomed me to his home. I only half-heard him, though, because I was focused – and not in a good way – on the guest of honor.

"Andrew Curtis," the President said, "may I present the hereditary princess of Iceland, Ingrid Ingunnardottir."

She was the beautiful blonde devourer from my nightmare. "Hello, Webb," she said, taking my hand. "I've heard so much about you." As soon as our fingers touched, I recognized her – not just as the woman in my dreams, but her signature. Or rather, her goddess's signature. The one I'd seen in my mother's timestream.

I felt as if I had dropped into another nightmare. Ingrid let go of my hand, and there was the President, introducing her to my mother. Ingrid reached out a hand toward her, a cruel smile on her lips. "No!" I yelled, in slow motion, and put out my own hand to bat Ingrid's away.

Too late. Too late! Their fingers touched, and then their palms.

And nothing happened.

Mom's head swiveled toward me. "Webb, are you all right? You look as if you've seen a ghost." She was still holding hands with Ingrid – who was now looking at me, too, her head cocked in a faintly quizzical manner.

"Fine. Sorry. Hot in here," I muttered. Then I rallied. "Ingrid, my apologies. I'm honored to meet you, and I hope my momentary lapse won't endanger relations between our nations. Or anything. Uh, I'm going to get something from the bar. Mom?"

"Sure," said Mom. "Club soda with lime."

"On its way," I said, and beat a retreat.

As I waited at the bar for our drinks, Roman sidled up to me. "What did you see back there?" he asked quietly.

I leaned away from him. "Why?"

He leaned in. "Because my brother's in love with her. But I dunno." He shook his head. "There's something funny about her."

I looked over my shoulder, where Mom was still chatting with Ingrid. And now I saw how Rex kept giving her fleeting glances. More than once, she returned his glance.

"I wouldn't worry," I said lightly. "She's probably his flavor of the month. She'll go back to Iceland and he'll fall for someone else."

As soon as I said the word "fall," I heard gasps all around us. I looked back again, just in time to see Mom take two slow steps away from the receiving line, then drop.

Antonia and I reached her at the same time. I helped her to a sitting position as Antonia clucked over her and called for her husband to get their physician. Cameras clicked again; I expected we'd be the top story on tonight's news.

"No doctors," Mom said crossly. "I'm fine. I just took a tumble, that's all – it happens when you're old. Thank you, Roman." She took her drink from his hand and sipped.

"Yeah, thanks, buddy," I said, accepting my own from him.

"I'm here to help," he said, in a more serious tone than I'd ever heard him use before. "Remember that."

"Roman," said his mother. "Go distract people with your guitar or something. Let's get you into a chair, Naomi." She nodded at me. I took my mother under one arm, Antonia got her other side, and on the count of three, Mom was back on her feet. Then I guided her to a chair and sat next to her.

"What happened?" I whispered in her ear.

"It *is* hot," she said, pitching her voice so that people nearby could hear her.

I played along. "It is," I agreed, at the same volume.

"I don't know what came over me," she said.

I looked away, the crowd parted, and there was Ingrid Ingunnardottir. She licked her lips.

"Mom, we need to get out of here," I said, my voice low.

She sighed. "Yeah, I know. But let me finish my club soda first. We need to make it look good."

I nodded. "Want something to eat?" I said, raising my voice to slightly-louder-than-normal again.

"Oh, no, I'm fine. But you should go."

"You're sure you'll be okay?"

"I'm. Fine," she said through clenched teeth. "Go."

So I went. Then, clutching my tiny plate, I made the rounds. As smarmy as Rex was, he was right about one thing: Cultivating support was a good idea. And here I was, in a roomful of heavy hitters. It couldn't hurt to start now to assemble a Plan B, in case I didn't get the grant I'd hung my future on.

The grant app. I pulled out my phone and checked the time. If I had any hope at all of submitting that app by the deadline, we needed to leave now.

I was stuffing my phone back in my pocket when a big, angry god loomed before me. "What have you done with Lucifer?" He growled at me.

"Hello, Loki," I said pleasantly. "Nice to see you here. Although I guess it's easy enough to get out for a turn around Earth when You control all the portals."

"Your attitude will not help you," He said. "Where is Lucifer?"

"Oh, was he one of Yours? He was running around loose, so I picked him up and put him in a playpen."

"You *what?*"

"Put him in a playpen," I said evenly, standing my ground against His fury. "And he's not getting back out again. Ever." I picked up a carrot from my plate and pointed it toward Ingrid Ingunnardottir. "She's one of Yours, too, isn't she?"

"No," He said, eyeing me sidelong. "She is Freya's."

I raised an eyebrow at Him, and cut a glance toward Ingrid. She was certainly beautiful enough to be allied with the Norse goddess of love, but she seemed to have one or two tricks up her sleeve that I'd never heard associated with Freya. Unhinging her jaws to swallow a man whole, for starters.

But I wasn't about to share my observation with Loki. "Interesting," I said instead. "So she'll reel in Rex to produce the heir, and Your control of humanity will be complete?" I waved the carrot in a warning gesture. "Seriously, Loki. I thought You knew better by now than to fuck with my family." Then I crunched it in His face.

He glowered at me, as if searching for a suitable comeback. Then He wheeled away and disappeared.

I shook my head and proceeded to where Mom still sat. "My work here is done," I said.

"That was Loki you were talking to, wasn't it?" she said rhetorically. "Don't ever believe anything He tells you."

"Don't worry," I said as I helped her to her feet. "I can always tell when Loki's lying."

Her mouth quirked up at one corner. "How?"

"His lips are moving. Come on." I gave her my elbow, and we proceeded to give our regrets to the President, Antonia, and Rex. Ingrid was deep in discussion with a bunch of fawning middle-aged men, which suited me just fine. I caught her eye and threw her a salute, and watched her expression harden. The game was on, and she knew it.

We waited fifteen minutes I didn't have for the valet to retrieve Dad's car. Then I flew like a demon to Golden. As I maneuvered the SUV through city traffic, I spared a glance at Mom. Her eyes were dull, and deep lines of pain creased her forehead and cheeks.

I took her hand, squeezed it, and said, "What did she do to you?"

She must have forgotten she had an audience; as soon as she felt my touch, she perked up. "What did who do to me?"

"Come on, Mom, don't play dumb with me. You know who I mean. Ingrid."

She smiled. "Lovely young woman, isn't she? Rex seems taken with her."

"Mom!" I said, and dropped her hand. "What did she do to you? You shook hands with her, and five seconds later, you were on the floor!"

She looked at me, baffled. "She didn't do anything, Webb. I tripped and fell. I told you that."

I gave up trying to swerve around a slow-moving truck and levitated over him instead. "Look," I said, when the truck was half a block behind us. "I got a whiff from her when I shook her hand. I think she may be involved with the goddess who's making you sick."

"Who is?" Mom asked.

"Ingrid!" I yelled. "Gods, Mom, what's gotten into you?"

"Don't shout at me," she said in irritation, and reclined her seat.

I gave up trying to get anything out of her, and concentrated on driving.

Ten minutes later, we were at the homestead. I hustled Mom into the house, dropped a kiss on her forehead, and said, "Gotta go. Thanks for an interesting day."

"Just a minute," she said, and ambled off toward her office, which was tucked away behind the stairs in the back of the house.

"Mom," I said, following her, "I have to go. The grant app is due by five o'clock, and I still have to pick up Dad."

"Just a minute," she repeated. "Would you pull that book down for me?"

I plucked it from the shelf while she gathered some other materials. "*Akak'stiman?*" I asked, reading the title. "What's this?"

"The classic work on Blackfoot mediation techniques. Here." She dumped three other books on top. "You need to study these."

I stared at her, dumbfounded. "What for?"

She placed both hands on her hips. "We have previously discussed that I'm dying, Webb. Have we not?"

I gulped. "Yeah. So?"

"But I still have to mediate the gods' new power-sharing agreement. And your sister is in no shape to help." She touched the book on the top of the stack. "So you're elected, whether you want to be or not."

"But I'm not a lawyer!" I protested.

"You don't have to be. All you need is the *cojones* to stand up to the gods – and don't tell me you don't have them. I watched you send Loki packing just a few minutes ago. I never could have done that at your age." A look of admiration flashed across her face, and then it was back to business. "Other than that, you need to know how to conduct a mediation. You've sat in on enough of my sessions over the years to have caught onto the basics; the rest is just conflict resolution theory, and that's what these books are for." She patted my arm. "You'll do fine."

"But why me?" I said. "You've been training people in these techniques for decades! Why don't you ask one of them to help you?"

"Because," she said, "you're the only one I can depend on." She put a hand to my cheek and pulled me down to her level so she could kiss me.

I was reminded of something I'd once heard Darrell say, about how the gods had dragged him off his chosen life's path, away from shamanism and toward a career as a Navy SEAL. For a long time, he'd been angry about the way the gods had meddled in his life – until he figured out a way to be both shaman and SEAL at once.

It was my mother yanking me from my chosen path – although it was certainly the fault of the gods. Regardless, I had a choice: I could be mad about it, or I could acquiesce, and then figure out later how to do both.

"Oh, all right," I said, and hugged her.

Traffic was bad all the way to Longmont, even in the air. Then Dad had to finish something he was working on before he could leave. I tried not to let my frustration show, even as I watched the minutes tick away.

At last, we were on the road again. I kept myself from checking the time every few seconds by filling in Dad on what had happened at the Holts'. But when I broached the topic of Ingrid, I hit the same wall I had with Mom. It was as if Someone was forcing them both to forget either the Icelandic woman or her goddess, or both.

I wondered if the same thing would happen if I brought up the subject with Aunt Shannon. If so, it would explain why she'd had trouble healing my mother. I made a mental note to call her as soon as I sent in the grant application.

Dad dropped me off at 4:50 p.m. I ran headlong into the house, dumped the books Mom had given me on coffee table, and tore back to my studio. "Come on, come on," I muttered as the desktop powered up. I had less than ten minutes until the deadline, and I still didn't know what I was going to write for that final question.

"Hey, honey," Hilary said from the door.

"Hey, baby." I gave her a distracted kiss. "Boy, have I had a crazy day. I'll tell you about it as soon as I get this thing out…the…" I plopped into the chair before my computer in surprise. The grant app showed it had been submitted at 4:00 p.m. – while I was cooling my heels at Dad's construction site. I pointed to the screen and said, "How…?"

"I sent it in for you," she said. "Your mom called after you left Golden. I knew you would be cutting it close, so I went ahead and submitted it."

I clutched her arm in panic. "But it wasn't done! I hadn't finished writing the last response."

In reply, she opened a file on the desktop and scrolled down. "I wrote it for you," she said.

> In the committee's view, art should have a lasting impact on society as a whole. What lasting societal impact do you envision for your installation?
>
> I often say that knitting is my superpower, and I'm only partly joking.

I come from a long line of people who do amazing things as a matter of course. I am their *heyoka* – their Sacred Clown. My mission in life is to make people laugh.

When I was a child, I did it all by instinct. But I have spent many years since then studying my craft, and I know now that laughter is necessary even when things look bleakest. Maybe especially when things look bleakest.

So I envision my project as a reminder to laugh. And the materials I plan to use will eventually dissolve and become one with the Earth again, as a reminder that all things pass away, good and bad alike. And even when good things pass away, they're making room for something even more wonderful.

When I was done reading it, I read it again. And again.

"Is it okay?" she asked, a hint of trepidation in her voice.

"It's perfect," I said in wonder. "But how did you…?"

She shrugged. "It's pretty much what you said in the meeting with Darrell yesterday morning. I just tweaked it a little, so I wouldn't give away any of your trade secrets." She dipped her head. "And I added that little bit of my own at the end. You haven't ever said it in so many words, but I know you believe it. And I believe it, too."

I closed the file and swept her into my arms. "I don't…" I began.

"Save it," she said, her fingers on my lips. "We're a team, remember?"

I kissed her fingers. "Of course, I remember. And I'm so glad you're on my side."

# Author's Note

I thought I was done writing about the Curtises, their offspring, and all their friends when I finished *Firebird's Snare*. But then fans said Webb deserved at least one book of his own. So I had a talk with the guy, and it turns out he's a very interesting fellow when his sister isn't overshadowing him. Plus there's clearly more to this story. So you can count on one more *Legacy* book later this spring.

As usual, I have to thank my crack editing team, Suzu Strayer and Kat Milyko, for keeping me from looking like a total idiot.

I found most of Webb's Navajo phrases at Omniglot.com. Here's a link to their Navajo page: http://www.omniglot.com/language/phrases/navajo.php

By the bye, *my hovercraft is full of eels* is, of course, a line from the classic Monty Python sketch about a dirty Hungarian phrasebook (which you can view here: https://youtu.be/G6D1YI-41ao). Omniglot.com considers it such a vitally useful phrase that it lists its translation in nearly 150 languages, including Pig Latin, Quenya (one of Tolkien's Elven languages), and Klingon. You can see them all here: http://www.omniglot.com/language/phrases/hovercraft.htm. How would Webb have known the line? I can only conclude that his parents raised him right.

To get the first word on all of my new releases, please click here to sign up for my spam-free newsletter. I'll also post the info at my blog and on my Facebook page, but the newsletter is your guaranteed way to find out what's coming up.

One more thing: If you enjoyed *Spider's Lifeline* – or even if you didn't – won't you please go back where you purchased the book to post a review? Reviews are a key way that readers find good books, and I treasure each and every review that my books receive. Thank you in advance!

Lynne Cantwell
April 2016

## About the Author

Lynne Cantwell writes mostly urban fantasy and paranormal romance, with a dash of magic realism when she's feeling more serious. She is also a contributing author for Indies Unlimited. In a previous life, she was a broadcast journalist who worked at Mutual/NBC Radio News, CNN, and a bunch of other places you have probably never heard of. She has a master's degree in fiction writing from Johns Hopkins University. Currently, she lives near Washington, D.C.

### The Pipe Woman Chronicles Universe

*Seized: Book One of the Pipe Woman Chronicles*
*Fissured: Book Two of the Pipe Woman Chronicles*
*Tapped: Book Three of the Pipe Woman Chronicles*
*Gravid: Book Four of the Pipe Woman Chronicles*
*Annealed: Book Five of the Pipe Woman Chronicles*
*The Pipe Woman Chronicles Omnibus*

*Where Were You When: A Land, Sea, Sky Anthology*
*Crosswind: Land, Sea, Sky Book 1*
*Undertow: Land, Sea, Sky Book 2*
*Scorched Earth: Land, Sea, Sky Book 3*
*The Land Sea Sky Trilogy*

*Dragon's Web: Book 1 of the Pipe Woman's Legacy*
*Firebird's Snare: Book 2 of the Pipe Woman's Legacy*
*Spider's Lifeline: Book 3 of the Pipe Woman's Legacy*
*(Book 4 coming Summer 2016)*

*A Billion Gods and Goddesses: The Mythology Behind The Pipe Woman Chronicles*

## Stand-Alone Novels

*SwanSong*
*The Maidens' War*
*Seasons of the Fool*

## Contributor

*Indies Unlimited 2012 Flash Fiction Anthology*
*Indies Unlimited 2013 Flash Fiction Anthology*
*Indies Unlimited 2014 Flash Fiction Anthology*
*Indies Unlimited Tutorials and Tools for Prospering in a Digital World*
*Indies Unlimited Tutorials and Tools for Prospering in a Digital World, Vol. II*
*BookGoodies How to Write A Book*
*First Chapters*
*13 Bites*
*Summer Dreams*
*Boo!: Volume 2*
*Winter Tales*
*Plan 559 from Outer Space*
*Other Realms*
*13 Bites Vol. III*
*I Heard It on the Radio*

## Find Lynne on Teh Intarwebz

Facebook: http://www.facebook.com/pages/Lynne-Cantwell
Twitter: http://twitter.com/lynnecantwell
Google Plus: http://plus.google.com/+LynneCantwell
Goodreads:
http://www.goodreads.com/author/show/696603.Lynne_Cantwell
Blog: http://www.hearth-myth.com

www.ingramcontent.com/pod-product-compliance
Lightning Source LLC
Chambersburg PA
CBHW071241130626
46556CB00003B/1107